The Mail-Order Bride

by

Daris Howard

Happy Mother's Day
from the
Howards
"2013"

The Mail-Order Bride

by

Daris Howard

Publishing Inspiration LLC

The Mail-Order Bride

by

Daris Howard

Copyright © 2004
by
Daris W. Howard

ISBN-10: 1480200387
ISBN-13: 978-1480200388

www.publishinginspiration.com

Publishing Inspiration LLC

This book is dedicated to my wife Donna. I would be lost without her.

Chapter 1
The Package

"Come on, Jim! Hurry! Hurry!" Eli yelled back over his shoulder, as he hurried along.

Jim came along, moving sprightly for an old man who walked with a cane. "I'm a-comin'. I'm a-comin'. I'm not as young as I once was, you know."

Eli was as giddy as a child waiting for Christmas. "This is the big day and I don't want to be late."

Jim laughed sarcastically. "Late? Ha! You're about two years late, if you ask me."

"Nobody asked you. You know I didn't have a choice."

"You always have a choice. It's just the consequences you don't get to choose, once you make the choice."

"You know I would have brought her with me, if I had had the money," Eli said.

Jim shook his cane at his young friend. "And I know that anyone who would leave his fiancée to go to another country and work is more than a little bit crazy."

Eli was too absorbed in his excitement to pay attention to Jim. As Jim continued his barrage, Eli put his hand to his forehead and scanned the horizon. No ship was yet in sight, but, with the crooked shoreline, a ship could almost be at the harbor before it came into view.

It was a typical May morning in Newfoundland. The sky was clear, promising a beautiful day. The sun was not yet up, but from its position below the horizon, it was casting a bright orange flame into the sky. The dawning colors, along with the fleeing shadows of the night, gave the awakening day a sense of excitement. The cool aroma that lingered from the long, but now expiring winter, made the air fresh and exhilarating. The quiet lapping of the water along the shore was broken only by geese overhead, honking their way farther north.

Still mumbling under his breath, Jim eased himself onto an old crate that was sitting on the dock. "I can't believe I let you drag me down here at five-o-clock on a Saturday morning."

Looking past Jim, Eli saw a solitary figure approaching the dock. "Here comes Whitman. I'll ask him about the boat's arrival."

He hurried toward Whitman, meeting him before he even got onto the dock. "Mr. Harris, I was wondering if you could boat me what tell the time is coming in?"

Whitman waved his hand and drawled, "Calm down, boy. You're

making no sense at all." Whitman, who never seemed to get excited about anything, put his hand on Eli's shoulder. "Now, why don't you start over."

Eli took a deep breath. "This is the big day!"

"Oh, is the bell for the church supposed to arrive today?" Whitman asked.

"It's more important than that," Eli replied as they continued to walk across the dock.

"More important than the church bell?" Whitman asked. "Is that shipment of toilet paper arriving? It's been a pretty rough road since we ran out. Pretty much defoliated the whole town."

By this time they had reached Jim, and he couldn't be outdone by Whitman's tale and had to come up with one better. He and Whitman started to swap tales about the tough times they had lived through. Eli knew these tales well - Jim and Whitman often exchanged them, each trying to outdo the other. He also knew that each time he heard them, the tales seemed to get bigger and more exaggerated. Eventually, they would get so exaggerated that Eli wasn't sure any of it was true at all.

Eli stood patiently, trying not to interrupt, but, by the time they got to the "great snowstorm", he could feel his tension beginning to rise.

"...and we had to all gather in the town hall to keep warm," Jim reminisced. "All we had to eat was chili, day after day. Why, no one dared light a match for fear they would blow us all to Halifax!"

Finally, Eli could stand it no longer. "Gentlemen! Gentlemen! We didn't gather here to talk about toilet paper or chili or any other matter of a worldly nature. We were talking about my future wife! My fiancée is coming today!"

"Your fiancée?" Whitman asked.

"Oh, you know," Jim groaned, "The young lady he put on hold to come to America."

"I didn't put her on hold," Eli said. "With the recession hitting in 1920, I couldn't find work, and we just didn't have enough money for both of us to come. We just..."

"...just decided I would go ahead and earn the money to bring her over," Jim said sarcastically, finishing the sentence for him. "Yeah, yeah, we've heard it a thousand times. But it's just like I always said, 'Absence makes the heart go yonder.' "

Whitman frowned. "I think the statement is, 'Absence makes the heart grow fonder.' "

Jim defiantly shook his finger at Whitman. "You think of it your way and I'll think of it mine."

"But you're wrong, Jim," Eli insisted. "I have written to her every week, and today she is going to step off of that boat and...

"...and into your arms to dance off into the sunset to live happily ever after," Jim said, rolling his eyes.

"I didn't say it was going to be perfect," Eli replied. "I was just saying we will finally be together again."

"What if this here Molly don't like it here?" Jim asked.

Eli smiled. "I'm sure she'll love it. I've been telling her all about it, and she's really excited to meet everyone."

Eli could see by the look on Jim's and Whitman's faces that they were still skeptical. Northshore was a tough town, full of lumberjacks, sailors, and only a few families. The people were free and independent and spoke their mind for good or bad.

Jim scowled. "And what I think is that you ain't told that Molly everything about this place. She might step off of that boat, take one look around, and get herself right back on it."

"I told her the people here are different than people back home, but that she will learn to love them like I have," Eli said.

Jim poked his young companion with his cane. "So what have you told her about me?"

Eli grinned and patted Jim on the shoulder. "I told her that I live with an old lumberjack that acts ornery to cover his big heart."

"Well, you ain't so easy to live with yourself, you know," Jim growled, brushing off any kind of compliment.

Eli shook his head and turned back to Whitman. "So, Whitman, do you have any idea when the ship should arrive?"

Whitman shrugged. "I thought you said it was today."

"Yes. Yes. It is supposed to come in today. But what time?"

"Hard to tell exactly," Whitman said, scanning the horizon. Then, remembering his clipboard, he looked down at it and then back at Eli. "What's the name of the ship?"

Eli pulled a paper from his pocket. "It's right here in this letter. It's kind of a strange name. *Nacs*, I guess."

"Nacs?" both Whitman and Jim repeated in surprise.

"Yes. N-A-C-S," Eli said spelling it for them.

Whitman shook his head. "I haven't ever heard of such a ship. But let me check the log." Whitman checked and shook his head. "Nope. The only ship I show scheduled for today is one called the *North Atlantic Cattle Ship*. I don't see any passenger boats coming until a week from tomorrow."

Eli flopped dejectedly onto a crate near Jim. "But the letter said she would be in today."

"Well," Whitman said. "I don't know about that. All I know is what my book says."

Jim looked at his disappointed young friend and seemed to soften. "Are you absolutely sure it was today, Eli?"

"Here. Read it," Eli said holding out the letter. Jim coughed and rolled

3

his eyes, and Eli remembered Jim couldn't read. "Oh. Sorry. Let me read that part to you. 'Dear Eli. Have booked passage on a ship called *NACS*. Watch for your bride on May 15. Molly.'"

Whitman frowned. "Kind of a strange letter!"

"I'm sure she was just in a hurry," Eli said.

A horn sounded in the distance, and all three men turned to see a ship coming into view from the south. They watched it for a while, as it steamed toward them, looming larger and larger.

Although the port at North Shore wasn't big, it was quite protected and deep, allowing ships to come right into the docks. The ships that came were usually medium-sized freighters, bringing items for the small towns along the coast that had shallower harbors. Many also brought items for the lumber camps and smaller towns inland. They usually left with loads of timber. Fishing ships often docked there overnight on their way to Grand Bank. Passenger ships only came a couple of times per month, since very few people came or left from there.

As the ship maneuvered into position along the freight dock, the words 'North Atlantic Cattle Ship' could be seen on the side. It was as big a freighter as ever came to North Shore. The rust along the bow indicated it was an older ship. The flag flying from the mast was not one that Eli recognized.

Whitman turned back to the other men. "Well, I'm sorry to disappoint you about your fiancee', Eli, but with the cattle boat coming in, I'll be needed to help it dock and check passports, papers, and such."

With that, Whitman headed on over to the freight dock, leaving a discouraged Eli slumped on an old crate.

Jim stood and kindly walked over and patted Eli on the shoulder. "Son, you know, it's none of my business and all, but do you think there is any way that Molly would let you down?"

A little bit of life returned to Eli as he shook his head. "No. I remember the night before I left. It was a clear evening in late May, almost exactly two years ago. A cool breeze was blowing, and the stars shone overhead. In the moonlight, I had taken her in his arms, and she had promised to wait for me until I could send for her. I can still almost feel her in my arms as if it was yesterday."

Eli's voice wandered off as he dreamily though of Molly. Jim continued to try and buoy up Eli's spirits, but was interrupted by Whitman coming down the dock with a burly man. The man stood a head taller than Whitman, who was no slouch himself. The man was wearing a captain's hat and a blue, double breasted wool coat. He had a rough beard and a stern expression. A pipe hung loosely between his teeth. Whitman pointed toward Eli as they approached. "This is the man you're looking for."

The man came over to Eli and glared down at him from his towering height. He eyed Eli with a disapproving scowl, pulling the pipe from his mouth. "So, you the man who ordered package. You look like decent enough fellow. Just as I figured."

"What are you talking about?" Eli asked. "I didn't order a package."

"Oh, don't try play innocent with me!" the captain's voice boomed, shattering the stillnes of the morning. "Me know your type. Outside, you look like good man. Inside, you sneaking devil."

"What?" Eli asked. The captain just scowled, and didn't say anything, so Eli turned to Whitman. "Whitman, what is this man talking about?"

Whitman shook his head. " I can't say I have the slightest idea."

The captain shook his finger at Eli, leaning right into his face, his own face livid. "Me told to deliver package to you safely, unharmed! Me not like, but do as told!"

Eli was more confused. "What package?"

The captain growled. "As if you didn't know!" Then, turning back in the direction of his ship, he shouted, "Hokay! Send her down!"

All of the men turned and watched as a woman started down the plank. She was dressed in drab black and brown from her head to her feet. She had a well-worn coat over her tired dress. She looked like a walking silhouette - a black burka veiling all of her face except for her eyes.

"Wow, who died!?" Jim gasped.

Slowly the woman approached them - slowing even more as she came. She stopped a good distance away, but, even still, it was easy to see that her clothes were dirty, and a smell of cattle wafted from her on the breeze. She stood there silent and motionless.

Eli looked at the captain, then at the girl, then back to the captain. "Well, where's the package?"

The captain pointed at the girl, more than a little annoyed. "Dis is package!"

Eli walked up to the girl, who immediately started to back away from him. "Okay," he said. "Give me the package."

The captain let out an exasperated gasp and threw his arms in the air. Jim began to understand what the captain was saying and walked over to Eli, placing his hand on his shoulder. "No, Eli. I think the captain is saying the girl *is* the package."

For an instant, Eli looked confused. Then, suddenly, his face lit up. He turned to the girl. "Molly? Molly!" He took another step toward her, and she took a step back. "Why, Molly," he continued not seeming to notice her timidness, "in all those old clothes I didn't recognize you. And I didn't expect you to come in on a cattle boat. It's been so many years. Let me look at you."

Eli reached up and swiftly pulled the veil from her face, as she shrank fearfully away from him. He looked at her and then back at the men, shock written all over his face. Then he turned back to look at the girl cowering before him. He was bewildered as he turned again to the men. "There's got to

5

be some mistake. This isn't Molly!"

Whitman stepped forward to get a better look at her. "What do you mean this isn't Molly? The captain said she was sent to you."

"Don't you think I would know my own fiancée when I see her?"

Jim snickered. "It has been two years."

Frustration sounded in Eli's voice. "This isn't Molly!"

Whitman walked all around the girl, looking her over. "Well, if this isn't Molly, who is she?"

Eli turned to the girl. "Miss, what is your name?"

"Her name is..." the captain started to say, but was interrupted by Eli. "I think she can speak for herself." Then, turning back to the girl, he asked, "Miss?"

The girl spoke quietly, her voice quivering. "Is permitted for woman to speak in presence of men?"

Eli nodded. "Of course it is. So what's your name?"

"Anya," the girl said quickly, then started to withdraw from the men again.

Eli grabbed her arm. "Don't be nervous. We won't hurt you. Can you tell us why you were sent here?"

Anya reached inside her coat and pulled out a piece of paper. "Have letter."

She handed the letter to Eli, then quickly escaped to a safe distance away. As Eli unfolded the letter, the other men crowded around. As he read it, Eli let out a gasp. "This is impossible!"

Jim shook his cane at Eli. "Are you going to let us in on all of this, or are we gonna sit around guessing all day?"

Eli, looking like he might collapse, flopped onto a crate as his face went white. He handed the letter to Jim. "Here, read it yourself."

Jim shoved the letter at Whitman. "Would you read the durned thing?"

Whitman started reading, chuckling to himself, "Well I'll be. The nerve of..."

"I meant out loud, you lowlife sea serpent!" Jim bellowed.

Whitman glared at Jim, but started to read. "'Dear Eli. I'm sorry I didn't have the courage to tell you this before. I could not come to you since, you see, I am married to Jack Taylor.'"

"Who's Jack Taylor?" Jim interrupted.

Eli looked up at the men, and spoke, his voice betraying his discouragement. "He's the postman back in the town I came from."

Jim burst out laughing. "You mailed her a letter every week, and she ended up marrying the postman who delivered 'em!"

Eli scowled. "I don't see the humor in this."

Whitman waved the letter. "May I continue?" Jim and the captain nodded, so Whitman continued reading. "'We have been married most of a year now and have a little boy. We named him Eli after you. You will be his godfather.'"

Jim, barely holding back his laughter, spoke dryly. "Oh, that should make you feel better."

"Would you let me finish?" Whitman snapped. Jim nodded, and Whitman read on. "'I've heard how in the West there aren't many women.'"

"Not the marrying type, anyway," Jim agreed.

Both Whitman and the captain said, "Shush," then Whitman continued, hurrying on before he could be interrupted again. "'I found an ad for a young lady. I am sending her to you. I'm sure she will be a good wife. Your friend, Molly.'"

Jim could contain himself no longer. He hooted. "A mail-order bride! Your *friend* Molly sent you a mail-order bride!"

The captain was shocked. "You never order young lady?"

"Of course not," Eli said. "Human beings are not property to be ordered through some magazine!"

The captain was now much subdued. "That's not what her father say. He say she good girl and bring good price."

"You mean she was sold by her own father?" Whitman asked.

"Da," the captain replied. "He tell me he get twenty-five dollar for her because she know English and is good cook."

"Wait a minute," Eli said, some realization setting in. "You mean that the money I sent to Molly was used to buy a bride for me?"

"And pay passage on boat," the captain said.

Jim looked narrowly up at the captain. "How much did she have to pay for a cattle boat ticket?"

"Boat ticket cost fifty dollar."

"Fifty dollars!" Eli exclaimed. "Why did Molly book her passage on a cattle boat? I sent her over two hundred dollars!"

The captain whistled. "Two hundred dollar! Me think she must keep most of it. Me think you lucky not have such a girl!"

"But I can't believe Molly would pay money for someone, as if she were a package that could be bought and sold," Eli said. Then he looked up at the captain. "And where did she stay on such a boat among all of the men?"

"She sleep with cows."

"You made her sleep with the cows?" Eli asked.

The captain was indignant at the accusation of mistreatment. "No other bed! We not passenger boat. And she not like to be around people."

"We could just sit around jabbering all day about things we can't change," Whitman cut in, "but we have a bigger question now. What do we do with her?"

Eli turned to Whitman. "What do you mean what do we do with her? The captain can take her back and tell her father there was a big mistake."

The captain's voice thundered. "I no want to take back! I charge hundred dollar boat ticket to take back!"

This upset Eli. "I don't have a hundred dollars. I sent every last cent I had to Molly."

The captain folded his arms. "No boat ticket, no take back."

"Now, be reasonable," Eli said. "I didn't ask for her, and..."

Jim grabbed Eli's arm. "You're forgetting something else, Eli. You were just saying how bad it was for Molly to send her on a cattle boat, but you are about to do the same thing."

Eli looked at the frightened young lady. "Well, well, maybe..." Eli stammered, trying to think of something. Suddenly, his face brightened. "Whitman, you're the mayor here. Maybe you can help find her a place to stay and a job."

Whitman scowled. "Now, hold on here just a minute. I may be mayor, but I am also the customs officer. The law has changed since you came over here, Eli. No one comes in unless they meet the new legal standards."

"What new legal standards?" Eli asked.

"In order to be a citizen, she must have a relative here," Whitman replied.

"But there is no way she could have a relative here," Eli said.

Jim pushed his way past Eli to Whitman and spoke as if in a whisper, but obviously loud enough for Eli to hear. "A husband would count as a relative. Isn't that right, Whitman?"

"Why, yes," Whitman grinned, as both he and Jim eyed Eli. "Yes, a husband would work nicely."

It took Eli just a second, but he quickly realized what they were thinking. "Oh, no. If you think I'm going to just up and marry someone I don't even know, you are dead wrong!"

Whitman chuckled. "Well, as I see it, you have one of two choices. You can send her back, or you can marry her. Either way, she's your responsibility."

Eli began to object. "Now, wait a minute! I didn't order her, and I..."

The captain interrupted. "Oh, one thing forgot. When marry, must send father Gratitude Dowry."

"Gratitude Dowry?" Eli asked.

"How you say, tip."

"If she stays, I'm supposed to send her father a tip?" Eli asked.

"Da. Very important custom. It tell how much you think she truly worth."

"And just how much is this 'tip'?" Jim asked.

"It depend. If not think good, you send dollar. If good, two or three dollar. Extremely good, perhaps four or five."

Jim looked over at Anya, the smell of the cows emanating from her. "I think a dollar should do it."

Whitman spoke to the captain. "What if he doesn't send anything?"

"When send tip, she considered acceptable to her village. If you no send tip, then she disowned in village."

Eli could hardly believe what he was hearing. "You mean that we are supposed to send back money for what we think she's worth, and if we don't, her village will disown her?"

The captain nodded. "Da."

A determined, defiant look came over Eli's face. "I won't do it! In the Bible, Isaiah said, 'I will make a man more precious than fine gold.' How then can I reduce a human being to the worth of three or four dollars?"

"I beg you consider," the captain said. "If you not send, village think her worthless and she feel worthless. She actually very nice."

"I won't do it!" Eli said.

Whitman pointed his pencil at Eli. "You may want to consider everything, before making a decision."

Eli looked lost and confused. He turned to Jim. "Jim, what am I to do?"

The old man stood quiet and stoic for quite some time, looking out to sea, as if considering many things. Finally, he turned to Whitman. "Isn't there something we can do while Eli considers his options?"

Whitman tapped his pencil more forcibly on his clipboard. "Well, she can either stay on the ship, or I can lock her up."

"She no stay on ship," the captain said, "for I no plan take back."

Eli again looked over at Anya standing there, quiet and scared, her fate being discussed as if she weren't even present. She was even more the victim here than he was. He spoke quietly to Whitman. "You can't lock her up. It's not right. She hasn't done anything wrong."

Whitman stopped tapping his pencil and pointed it at Eli. "I'm just following the law."

Jim poked Whitman with his cane. "It seems to me the law can be bent a little bit here."

Whitman pushed the cane away. "I can't break the law."

Jim turned the can back and gave Whitman another prod. "We didn't say break it! We said bend it! Like you did when your nephew was caught stealing candy from the..."

"Okay, okay!" Whitman interrupted. "Maybe we can give a little. We could let her stay here as long as the captain is in port. That would give Eli some time to make a rational decision."

"But where she stay?" the captain asked. "She no stay on ship."

Jim lowered his cane and leaned on it. "She can't stay with us. What would the town folk say?"

"Heaven knows what they'll say anyway," Eli groaned.

Jim pursed his lips, looking narrowly at Whitman. "That leaves only one place."

Whitman realized what Jim was meaning, and pointed his pencil at him. "Now, wait just a minute! I never volunteered to..."

"Oh, come on, Whitman," Jim said, jerking the pencil out of his hand and pointing it back at him. "All your children are gone, and you rumble around in that big house of yours like a musketball in a cannon."

"What would my wife think?" Whitman asked.

"You know Agnes," Jim said, "and you know that if you put anyone else in charge of this girl, you're gonna be in big trouble."

Whitman looked at Anya. "But she's so, so..."

"Dirty?" Jim added the word for him. "So would you be if you had slept with cows for a month. I'm sure Agnes could find a dress or something and make her look almost human."

Whitman scanned around the circle of men. He jerked his pencil back from Jim. "Oh, all right!" He tapped Eli on the chest with the pencil. "But you better hurry up and make up your mind, Eli Whittier! I'm giving you until the captain leaves port which is, which is..." He looked at the captain questioningly. "One week from tomorrow," the captain said.

Whitman turned back to Eli. "Which is one week from tomorrow. That's all! Got it?"

Eli nodded bleakly. "Yes. Yes."

Whitman shook his head. "I'll go get Agnes and try to explain this to her. Heavens, I don't even understand it all myself!" He turned and headed toward his home. He was still shaking his head and was walking at an unusually fast pace.

They watched Whitman disappear toward town, then the captain stuck out his hand to Eli. "My name is Victor." Eli shook the captain's hand, and then Jim did. The captain continued, "I must be getting back to my work. I will go get her things."

With that, he headed back to his ship. For a brief moment, everything was quiet except for the lapping of waves and the cargo crane starting to move crates to the dock. Jim looked from Eli to Anya, then back at Eli, and burst out laughing. "A mail-order bride! The preacher got a mail-order bride! I thought I'd heard it all." He smiled slyly at them. "Perhaps I should leave you two alone. After all, the guys down town haven't heard the news."

As Jim started thumping his way across the dock toward town, Eli panicked at the thought of being alone with this strange girl and not knowing what to say. "No, Jim, don't leave! Jim, I..."

But Jim just turned, pushed Eli back toward Anya with his cane, and, with a laugh, continued on his way.

Eli forced a glance toward Anya. She shyly lifted her eyes to meet his and quickly lowered them again. She had already wrapped her veil back into place so her eyes were all that Eli could see, but they spoke volumes.

Eli felt sorry for her, but he struggled with his own feelings about Molly. He tried to put his feelings aside for a moment and think of Anya and what she must be feeling. He began to speak, but stumbled over his words. "I, uh, I mean..."

Anya's voice trembled. "Send Anya home?"

"Well, I don't know if that's possible, but it would probably be best."

"No like Anya?"

"I can't say I don't like you. I don't even know you."

Anya voice was pleading. "Anya good cook. Anya work hard, learn cook, sew, learn English. Anya speak good English?"

Eli smiled at her. "Yes, you speak good English."

"Anya try hard make new owner happy."

"Call me Eli. I'm not your owner. A person can't own another person."

Anya's voice betrayed her confusion. "But father own Anya. Father sell, Eli buy. Now Eli own."

Eli turned away, looking out over the sparkling ocean. The sun was now peeking over the horizon, creating a prism across the water that seemed to travel to the sun and beyond. The sun's rays shot into the sky, crowning the distant edge of the earth with a sparkling tiara more beautiful than any queen's. The beauty of the day seemed to be in deep contrast to the heaviness he felt in his heart.

Eli's voice was quiet as he answered. "No, Anya. God made man in his own image. No man can really be owned by another."

"No man, but woman."

Eli turned back to face her. His voice was firm but kind. "No. He did not make a woman to be owned any more than a man."

"Anya not understand. If Eli think this, then why buy Anya?"

Eli lowered his eyes. "I didn't buy anyone. I sent money to Molly so she could come over."

"Mean buy Molly and get Anya by mistake and make Eli sad?"

Eli shook his head. "No. I did not send money to buy Molly. Molly was my fiancée. I sent money for her boat ticket."

"Oh. Already own Molly and send for her."

"No. I did not own Molly. She was my fiancée."

"But if fiancée, Eli own."

Eli felt the frustration welling up inside of him. It wasn't directed at Anya, because she was more of an innocent victim than he was. So at whom did he feel this anger? Was it at himself for believing and trusting Molly? Was it at Molly? But how could he feel upset at someone he had loved for so many years? He swallowed hard and took a deep breath. "No, Anya. I don't own anyone."

Eli could again hear the fear and discouragement fill Anya's voice when she spoke. "Then Eli send Anya back?"

Eli smiled gently. "Wouldn't you be happier back home with your own family?"

She turned to look at him. "Father beat Anya since not please owner. Sell 'nother owner."

Her eyes appeared to be pleading with him, begging him to understand something that was beyond his comprehension. For a brief moment, they looked directly into each other's soul. Her words sank into his heart. She lowered her eyes, and he turned and looked again out over the ocean as the sun burst fully into view above the horizon. His heart felt dark and heavy even as the day burst forth full of light. It was as if a new day was dawning but he wanted to hang on to the old day, the day when he still believed Molly was coming.

He didn't get to contemplate it all very long before the clump of shoes hitting the dock sounded behind him. He turned and saw Agnes Harris bearing down on him with Whitman strolling far behind at a leisurely pace. By the way Agnes was walking, and the scowl on her face, Eli knew she meant business. She glared at him but turned her attention to Anya.

"You must be the poor dear. Don't worry, now. Agnes will take care of you. You are off of that awful boat." She glared again at Eli as if aiming her words at him. "I will keep you safe from men who treat women like property!"

Eli was shocked at the accusation. "But I..."

Before he could defend himself, Mabel Jaimison and Elizabeth Jackson came running onto the dock, each trying to outpace the other. They ran over to Anya and started to fuss over her.

"Oh, here she is," Mabel cooed.

Elizabeth stepped between Mabel and Anya, wafting her hand in front of her nose. "To think of the poor child riding all that way on a cattle boat."

Agnes took command of the situation. "Come on, ladies. Let's get her cleaned up."

Eli knew he needed to clear things up. "Now, Mrs. Harris, I just wanted to explain that..."

Agnes turned and poked him in the chest with her finger. "As for you, sir, you will be expected at our house for dinner at precisely six o'clock."

"At your house?"

Agnes's voice was stern and harsh. "You don't think we would let you marry her until you've gotten to know her, do you?"

"Well no, but I..."

"Six o'clock sharp!" Agnes's thundered. "And don't you dare be late!"

With that, she hurried to catch up to the other ladies who were leading Anya off the dock toward town. Eli heard Mabel say, "Can you believe the nerve? And him the town preacher besides." He heard Elizabeth add, "I can't believe my eyes. And on a cattle boat, too."

Eli called after them, "I didn't order her. And who said I was going to marry..." but they were gone.

Whitman nonchalantly wandered onto the dock. Eli stood silently for a moment, watching the ladies disappear up the road, then slowly he turned back to Whitman. "Just what did you tell her?"

Whitman was the picture of innocence. "Me? I just told her that your mail-order bride came in, and she had to ride a cattle boat all the way here."

"But I didn't order her!"

Whitman grinned. "You wanted me to get Agnes to let her stay at our house, didn't you?"

"I didn't want you to make her think I ordered a mail-order bride! And why did you have to go telling Mabel and Elizabeth?"

"I didn't tell them. Agnes told Mabel on the way down here, and, I guess, Mabel must have told Elizabeth."

Eli groaned. "Now it will be all over town."

Whitman laughed. "Did you think there would be any way to stop that?"

Before Eli could even answer, Jim came shuffling onto the dock, laughing to himself. "I just passed the ladies taking Anya over to your place, Whitman. I haven't seen that much excitement out of them since old Mabel found out it was Mr. Tallcott, and not a weasel, who was stealing her chicken eggs."

"Whitman didn't tell them the whole story," Eli said. "He just told them my mail-order bride came in, and she had to ride on a cattle boat."

"Yeah," Jim said. "I told some of the boys down town that you had a mail-order bride come in."

Eli rolled his eyes. "Oh, and what did they have to say?"

Jim elbowed Eli. "That preacher's a sly devil, isn't he? I didn't think he had it in him." Then Jim burst out laughing.

"Oh, you guys have been a whole lot of help," Eli said. "And just how am I suppose to get up and preach a sermon tomorrow, when everyone thinks I ordered a mail-order bride?"

"Now, calm yourself down," Jim said. "Maybe you can just preach about..." Jim paused to think a moment, then continued, "about the evils of marriage."

Jim and Whitman both laughed, but Eli didn't. "I don't see the humor in this!" he snapped.

Victor approached carrying a small, ugly bag. "Here her things," he said, holding it out to Whitman.

Whitman took the bag and looked it over. "That's all she's got? There couldn't be much more than one change of clothes in there."

13

Victor shook his head. "I think she no have more clothes than what she wear. I think just things from home."

"I'll take this to her," Whitman said. "I'm sure she'll be wanting whatever's in here." Whitman then turned to Eli. "And, Eli, don't forget to be at our house for dinner. And I wouldn't be late. The way Agnes said it, it wasn't a request."

Whitman turned to leave, but stopped and turned back to Jim. "Oh, and Jim, you'd be invited to dinner, too."

Jim smiled. "Well, that's good for us. Agnes is a good cook."

Whitman nodded, and with that, he headed home.

Victor tipped his hat. "If you men will excuse, I have shipment to take care of." He gave a slight bow, then headed back to his ship.

"As for us, I think we better make sure the town folk are told the truth before rumors get out of control," Jim suggested.

"I bet it's too late for that," Eli muttered, as they headed for town.

Chapter 2
In Town

As they walked through town, Eli was very aware of people stopping, staring, and pointing. He was glad Jim didn't abandon him. He could remember more than once, when he was a boy, being abandoned by friends when things got rough. He could especially remember when some friends had talked him into throwing eggs at the carriage of the duke and, when all of them got caught, the other boys blamed it all on him and let him take it alone. His father met with the duke and worked out a deal for him to clean out the duke's stables as punishment. None of his friends helped him then, either.

But Jim was more than a friend. He was almost family. Jim didn't ever seem to care what people thought of him. He had an ability to take what people said and ignore it more than anyone Eli knew. Of course, Eli knew Jim had the ability to ignore advice that he probably should listen to.

Eli could remember the day he, himself, had stepped off of the ship in Newfoundland. He had planned to go to Pennsylvania and join the Quakers, like his mother had wanted, but their ship had gotten into a major storm that had blown them far off course.

Upon entering port, he wasn't even sure where he was, but, somehow, he felt God had brought him here, and, if God wanted him here, here he would stay. He had no food to continue on to Pennsylvania, anyway. His food had run out during the last few days of the voyage while they fought the storm. He had very little money and knew no one. He could remember how hungry he was. Scanning his new surroundings, he saw an old man standing on the end of the dock farthest out toward the sea. The man was standing alone, just staring out over the ocean.

Eli could remember how he was just about to head into town, when he again looked at the old man and felt drawn to him. Eli shouldered his pack and walked over. He introduced himself and asked if, by chance, the man knew where he could find a place to live and possibly some work and food. The old man had continued to stand motionless, except for the wind blowing through his white hair, not saying a word, as if he were transfixed by the storm-tossed waves.

The old man's tear-filled eyes seemed to search far beyond the distant horizon. Eli was just about to turn and head to town, when the old man had wiped his eyes and turned to face him. He had seemed startled as he looked Eli over, but finally he spoke. He said his name was Jim, and he had an extra room. Eli thought about how Jim had taken him home and had given him a meal of elk steak, potatoes, and collard greens. Eli couldn't remember a meal ever tasting so good in all of his life.

Since that day, their lives had become intertwined. Jim had become like a father to him. He had helped him with almost everything. It was Jim who helped him get a job at the lumber camp. Jim was probably the oldest man in the whole area. He knew everybody, and they knew him. That didn't mean they necessarily liked him; they just knew him. But Eli had grown to love Jim. He knew that under that rough exterior, he had a kind heart.

However, something seemed to be bothering Jim; something Eli could never quite put his finger on. Jim would never talk of his past, and Eli knew better than to mention it. Any questions of it had only been met with grunts of disapproval.

Now, as they walked toward the pool hall, which was one of the main social centers of the town, he was glad to have Jim by his side. Most people didn't make fun of Jim or contend with him on anything. Even though he was almost eighty, he had a natural wit about him that left most people who tried to confront him looking stupid. That, along with his grouchy demeanor, made people leave him alone. But not today. Word about the mail-order bride was already around town. Today, Eli and Jim were just too irresistible a target.

Janice Klampton, whose husband ran the only general store in town, came marching up to them, obviously intent on making a scene.

"What is this I hear, Eli Whittier, that you went and got yourself a mail-order bride?"

Eli was just about to explain it, but Jim spoke first.

"Well, of course, Mrs. Klampton, he had no choice."

"Oh, and just why is that?"

"You can't expect a fine young man like Eli to marry the kind of women that live around these parts. He needed to find a decent woman for a wife."

Mrs. Klampton was a large woman. In fact, large was too kindly a word for her. She was more like the size of a small battleship. She stood a good six inches above Jim and was nearly as wide as she was tall. Jim often said that if he were caught in the desert with a burning sun and no trees, he would want Janice Klampton to provide his shade. She pulled herself to her full height and glared down at them. Eli felt like crawling into a hole, but Jim stood firm as she glowered at him. "Just what are you inferring? I'll have you know that I have lived here my entire life."

"My point exactly," Jim answered.

As everyone around them burst into laughter, Mrs. Klampton spun indignantly on her heels and retreated back to the store. Eli wasn't so sure that Jim was helping his cause.

They finally reached the pool hall, which was connected to the bar. Although Eli didn't drink, and Jim had quit since Eli had come, they often sat and drank sarsaparilla, because it was a nice way to unwind and visit. Eli hadn't realized he had been any influence on Jim until, one day, the bartender

16

mentioned the fact that he only drank sarsaparilla now.

"Why don't you ever drink a man's drink anymore?" Bob, the bartender, had asked Jim, with Eli sitting right across from him. "The preacher man being too much of an influence on you?"

Jim didn't even flinch as he sipped his sarsaparilla. "Maybe I decided that when I grow up, I'd like to be a man like him, instead of like some I know."

Bob withdrew quickly to his place behind the bar as the laughter of the other men filled the room. No one had ever bothered them again after that, and the men in the pool hall soon accepted Eli for what he was. They seemed to respect him for it. Some of them even began coming to church. However, Eli wasn't sure but what their wives made them come.

Today, as they entered, everything went deathly still, and everyone turned to look at them. Eli felt more uncomfortable than he could ever remember being before. Jim didn't seem ruffled at all. They slipped into their usual table, which was empty, even though they almost never came in before evening. The morning crowd usually just sat around drinking coffee, but that didn't stop Jim from ordering two sarsaparillas.

No one said a word as Bob served them. Everyone was silently staring at them. Eli could feel his face getting warmer and warmer, and he just wanted to run, but Jim had convinced him that the only way to get word out was to start at the grass roots.

Jim drew in a good deep chug of sarsaparilla, swallowed with a gulp, and then sat back as relaxed as if nothing was unusual. "I suppose some of you might have heard Eli had a mail-order bride come in this morning," he said.

That was the bombshell that blew the dam apart. Immediately, everyone crowded around them asking questions. Eli couldn't even get the answer to one out before another was asked. Jim just sat quietly and watched Eli wriggle and squirm through it all. The place was getting fuller by the minute, and Bob was pleased to see his business booming on a Saturday morning. He brought over an extra sarsaparilla for Eli. "This one's on the house," he said. "One to drown your sorrows in." The men all laughed, and a look from Jim got him a free one, too.

As the men learned about what Molly had done, Tom Jaimison proposed a toast. "To all men everywhere who ever loved a woman, only to have her dump them."

All the men raised their cups and shouted, "Here, here!" and drank their coffee, while Eli and Jim sloshed down a couple more sarsaparillas provided by other good-hearted souls. It wasn't until Whitman showed up that any attention was turned elsewhere. Whitman wasn't a person to usually come down to the pool hall, and, being mayor, his presence made for a small uproar.

"What'll you have?" Bob boomed out, as Whitman settled himself at the bar.

"How about some ham and eggs and a glass of milk?" he answered back. "My wife kicked me out of the house and said she was too busy to make breakfast."

The men all laughed. "Getting that girl all dolled up for the preacher boy, huh?" Fred Jackson hollered, and all of the men guffawed again.

"Now, don't go drinking all of that milk at once," Bob said putting the plate of food in front of Whitman. "We don't want the mayor passed out at my place."

As the men roared with laughter, Eli thought this might be a good time to slip out unnoticed. "Hey, Preacher," Bob yelled after him, "I've got a good suit for when you're ready to get hitched. It would also work for a funeral."

Eli fled quickly out the door, the laughter still ringing in his ears. Jim went to pay the tab. "So, Jim, are you going to talk the preacher boy into marrying this girl?" Bob asked.

"If I can," Jim answered, "because we don't want him to leave. He might just be the best thing that ever happened to this town."

The men looked at each other quietly as Jim left. The town had changed a lot since Eli had come two years earlier, and they all knew it. Most of them teased him about his advocation of learning and religion. They said he got the women folk all stirred up, and some of them said their wives wouldn't let them go fishing on Sundays anymore. But, in reality, they all liked him and knew everyone was better off for him being there. Some had never thought about it, though, until that very moment, but each man knew he didn't want Eli to leave.

But, for Jim, there was more, much more.

Chapter 3
Molly

As he walked home from the pool hall, Eli could feel everything he drank sloshing back and forth in his stomach, and he felt nauseous. He wasn't sure, though, whether it was the soda or the feelings in his heart that made him sick. As soon as he arrived at the cabin he and Jim shared, he went to his room.

Eli could remember the first time he had come into this house. He had been so hungry, the smell of the already prepared food was so overwhelming that he could think of nothing else. Jim slid a pile of dirty clothes off of a chair for Eli and scooted it to the table.

Once Eli had finished eating, and sat back and looked around, he could tell this was the home of a bachelor. Clothes, most of them worn and dirty, were draped across chairs, tables, and everything else. Although it was nice, the house was dusty and cluttered, having had little or no care in years.

Jim cleared enough out of a second bedroom for Eli to sleep that night. It had a bed in it with a toy bear resting on the pillow and a beautiful, carved wooden horse on the floor beside it.

Eli wondered why an old bachelor would have a two bedroom house containing such things. When he inquired about it the next day, Jim had just grunted and quickly stored the toys out in a shed. Eli decided that Jim must have had people rent from him before, or something, but he wasn't sure. Over the next few days, Jim and Eli had worked to clean the house. He had soon learned not to ask too many questions; Jim didn't want to share much. Though he and Jim lived there comfortably together, he still knew so little about the man.

Now, as Eli sat down on the end of his bed, he picked up the only picture he had of Molly. It was just a hand-drawn sketch, but she seemed to be looking out of it at him all the way from England. He had always imagined that she was smiling at him, but now she seemed to be laughing. He threw the picture to the floor.

He pulled out the box of letters he had received from Molly through the last year, as well as the ones from his mother. How could he not have known Molly was married? It did take letters over a month, sometimes even two or three, to arrive, but it appeared she had been married more than a year.

He began reading. He started with the notes that would have been written shortly after he assumed Molly was married, and started working his way to the present. His mother was never one to tell anyone's news outside of the family, for fear she'd be gossiping. She did tell him how his brothers and sisters were doing. She told how his older brother, Jacob, and Jacob's wife

Marissa, had their first baby - a little girl. She was their pride and joy. The whole family spoiled her. Oh, how Eli wished he could be home - home in England. But could that really be home now? He had changed so much.

Then he spotted something in his mother's letter that he now understood differently. "Eli," his mother wrote in her letter, "with all that has happened with Molly, are you considering coming home?"

Home. The word echoed again in his head. Where was home? What was home? Could it be home when every dream he had there was gone? Much of what drew his heart there was now the same thing that was tearing it apart.

He thought of her words. He had known Molly had been sick, but now he realized that his mother thought he knew more than that.

He hunted until he found Molly's letter that had been penned near the same time. He read it. She was trying to hint she was married. The sickness wasn't the flu. It was more than that; that was obvious now. She wasn't coming right out and saying she was morning sick, but she was trying so hard to have him understand. Why hadn't she just said it?

For a moment, bitterness and anger filled his heart. How could they just let him go on believing? How could Molly do this to him? Eli read more and more letters. The more he read, the more he realized it was his own fault. He was far away and the love he had for Molly and the dreams they had shared were the strings that still tied him back to what he had known. He hadn't wanted to quit believing. It was easier to go on, ignoring the obvious. He was the one that couldn't give up his dream.

The tears started coming faster and faster. His emotions were a mixture of anger and sorrow. He could feel the turmoil in his heart. The love he felt for Molly was conflicting with the anger welling up from deep inside. Anger and love can't exist freely together, and his emotions battled back and forth.

He was reeling from this inner turmoil when Jim stepped inside his door. Eli turned his face away so Jim wouldn't see the tears. Jim didn't need to see them to understand. The letters were strewn on the floor with Molly's picture near them.

Jim stepped up and put his hand on Eli's shoulder. "Perhaps she didn't tell you because she still loved you."

"How could a person love another and do that to them?" Eli asked.

Eli reached down, picked up Molly's picture, and was just about to rip it to pieces when Jim pulled it quickly, forcefully, from his hands.

Jim's voice was stern and fatherly. "I'll take that."

"But Jim, she's gone out of my life for good."

"Yes, but she's still a memory, a good memory, and good memories can be hard to come by. I'll just hang on to this for a few days until you can think more clearly, and then if you still decide to rip it up, that will be your choice."

Eli knew it was no use arguing with him. He was right anyway, and Eli knew it.

Eli spent the day going through the letters and memories from home. Jim spent the day listening to Eli. Eli felt like the memories in his mind and the feelings in his heart were a jumbled mass of confusion, like puzzles dumped into one large pile. As he shared his feelings with Jim, it was as if the puzzles were sorting themselves out, though the puzzle was far from complete.

He felt like a man caught between two worlds. He didn't know if he could ever feel England was really home again, but was this home? He had thought it would be once Molly came and they were married. But now, that was never going to happen.

He began to realize that home was not as much a place, but a feeling - a feeling of everything being right with those around you. Things didn't seem right, and, with Molly gone out of his life, he wondered if they ever would be right again.

Chapter 4
Anya

The days were getting longer, but the sun was still quickly approaching the horizon as Eli and Jim headed for the Harris's house. Eli felt as though he was going to an execution - his own.

As they approached town, the air was full of circling seagulls hoping to get a free meal where the fishermen were cleaning their ships from the day's work. The evening air was filled with the cries of the birds fighting over every piece they could find, and the squawk of those left out of the fray.

The sounds of the last of the freight loading onto the cargo ships were slowing as many of the men headed to the pool hall for the evening. A few late ships that had struggled to find a good day's catch were straggling into port, blasting their horns - bragging their arrival.

As Eli and Jim entered town, with Eli dressed in his church-going clothes, people stared and pointed. Eli had hoped time would have worn off some of the ripeness of the news, but if it had, he couldn't tell. Jim walked briskly beside him, cane in hand, dressed in his Levi jeans and a flannel shirt. Jim didn't get much more dressed up than that for any occasion. Sometimes his old wooden cane was the dressiest part of his outfit. Jim had found a beautiful piece of wood with many decorative branches and a curve that was natural for a cane. He had trimmed off the branches and whittled faces into it, much like a portable totem pole. He didn't use his cane much for walking. He carried it more for whacking anything or poking anyone who drew his ire. Eli had been on the receiving end of that more times than he could count.

As they continued on down the street, Eli felt like he was in a circus parade. He was an unwilling clown that everyone came to gawk at. All that was missing were the peanut vendors and the elephants. Jim had his eyes set on one thing, the Harris's house on the far end of town, and nothing else seemed to distract him.

It seemed like hours before they finally reached the white picket fence leading to it. It was the only truly white picket fence in town. Whitman had ordered the wood in from St. John's. There were a few mimic fences, people trying to be like them, but they had rough, hand-cut boards that were white-washed, but always looking worn and in need of repair. Some things just weren't right without the original material.

As Jim opened the little wooden gate and started up the rock path to the wide porch, the smell of fried chicken engulfed them. Jim grinned at Eli. "Almost makes it worth it, doesn't it?"

Eli didn't think so, but he didn't say it. They approached the door, and Jim rapped heartily with his cane.

It was Whitman who opened the door. "Eli, Jim, good to see you. Come in. Come in." Whitman glanced at the clock on the mantle and smiled as he led them to some chairs. "You're even slightly early."

Jim tapped his cane on the floor. "Eli didn't want us to be late. He said he was already in enough trouble around town."

"It wasn't just me," Eli said. "Jim swore he could smell that wonderful fried chicken your wife makes clear over to our house."

Whitman smiled and patted his stomach "She is a good cook. Why, when we first married, if I stood sideways and stuck out my tongue, I looked like a zipper."

Jim looked at Whitman, standing a good six inches taller than anyone else in town, and still thin enough to "fit through a keyhole" as he often told Eli. "Now you've only become a wrinkled zipper," Jim mumbled.

Eli was anxious about matters at hand and wanted to get right to what he thought were more important issues. "Did you take some time to explain more to your wife about Anya?"

"I've got a few words in," Whitman replied. "It hasn't been easy. She and her lady friends have been running around, flitting here and there, getting this bow and that ribbon. Trying this dress on Anya, and that bow on Anya, and Anya this and Anya that." It wasn't hard to tell, by the tone of his voice, that he was more than a little annoyed.

"Well, it sounds like they like her," Jim said.

"I don't know about that," Whitman said, "but I do know that Eli better be careful what decisions he makes. I think they've become pretty protective of her."

Eli stood up, frustration filling his voice. "I just don't understand. I have tried hard to follow God's will. Why would God answer my prayer about my wife this way?"

"You remember how a few weeks ago you gave that sermon on how, when we pray, God answers our prayers through the efforts of someone else?" Jim asked.

"Why, yes," Eli replied. "I never thought you listened to my sermons."

"I try not to," Jim growled. Then he continued, "Anyway, think about it, Eli. Maybe she's not the answer to your prayers, but maybe you're the answer to hers."

"I don't understand," Eli said.

Whitman put his hand on Eli's shoulder. "You're the one who always says you feel that God will direct your life if you let him. Maybe He's directing yours now."

"And who knows," Jim added. "Maybe she *is* the answer to your prayers. You always say that God knows better how to answer our prayers than we do."

Eli grinned. "Maybe you two ought to get up and preach the sermon tomorrow."

Jim stood, laughed, and teasingly poked Eli with his cane. "No. I can't wait to see what kind of sermon you come up with. I bet, as the word gets out, you'll have a packed house."

Just then, Mabel and Elizabeth came running in. They ran to Eli, each grabbing one of his arms, trying to be the first to get his attention. Mabel pulled him around to face her as she spoke.

"Eli, are you ready to greet your future wife?"

Eli's face reddened. "Now, wait just a minute here. No one said that..."

He was interrupted by a loud clatter. He looked over at Jim and saw that he had dropped his cane to the floor and was staring, as if in a trance. Whitman, beside him, also stood motionless. Their faces had a look of astonishment. Eli turned around to see what drew their attention, and there stood Agnes with the most beautiful woman he had ever seen. It took just a moment for it to dawn on him that the woman was Anya.

She had gorgeous ebony hair that fell loosely down the length of her back to her waist - hair that highlighted her perfect, olive complexion. She stood tall and magnificent in a sky blue evening gown with puffy white sleeves that ended just below her shoulders. Her bare arms were strong, but feminine, though her hands looked calloused from years of hard work.

The dress was pulled tight around her body, revealing a wonderful, full figure and a slim waist that could not have shown in the clothes she wore when he saw her before. Her dress ended just above the ankle, showing just enough that Eli could tell she had attractive, slender legs. As Eli stood transfixed, she looked up at him momentarily, then, shyly, lowered her beautiful brown eyes.

Whitman was the first to speak. "She cleans up real nice, doesn't she?"

Eli continued to stare, mutely, until Jim nudged him. Then, unsure of himself, he moved slowly toward her. She timidly backed away. Agnes stepped up and took Anya's arm, linking it through Eli's. She then turned to the rest of the group. "Dinner won't be ready for a little while. Why don't we leave these two alone to get acquainted, and the rest of us will go in the kitchen to visit?"

Jim and Whitman stood motionless, as if still in shock. Agnes grabbed each of them by an arm. "I said kitchen!"

Jim, coming to himself, nodded and reached for his cane, "Oh, yes. Kitchen."

Eli felt frightened at being alone with Anya again and wanted to follow them. "But I don't think that..."

Jim poked him with his cane, pushing him back toward Anya. "Eli, do as your told."

Agnes herded everyone else away. As Jim and Whitman went off, they stole one more glance at Anya, then looked at each other, and each shook his head. Eli knew neither could believe this was the same girl that earlier in the morning had looked like a peasant and smelled like a cow.

Eli stood there for a moment, Anya's arm through his. He didn't know what to do, so he led her to the couch. She seemed unsure for a moment, but finally sat on the very end. Eli sat at the other end. Distance seemed to make the situation somewhat more comfortable.

The silence was deafening, so Eli decided to try to start a conversation.

"So, um, how was your voyage?"

"Fine."

"Did they treat you well? I mean, were the captain and his men nice to you?"

"Men feed Anya good, and not bother."

They sat quietly for another short, but eternal, amount of time. The tick-tock of the mantle clock was the only sound, seeming to pound like a timpani. Finally, Eli could stand it no longer and tried again. He turned to face her. "Anya. Anya, please look at me."

Anya turned slightly toward him, but did not look at him directly. "Anya, I think we're both confused and not sure what to do. Maybe you could tell me a little more about what life was like for you in your village?"

Anya's voice quivered. "Anya not know what say. Anya never speak to man before, except Father and brothers."

"Was that the way in your village?"

"Yes. Woman not speak to man not relative. And, then, only speak when spoke to."

"Are many women sold as brides?"

"All woman sold when age to marry."

"Were many sold through an ad like you were?"

"No. Anya first woman sold out of village. Father much progressive. Father say if daughter learn English and learn cook, do better outside village."

"Are you happy to be here?"

"Why not happy? Have much food. Have home."

"Would you not have food at home?" Eli asked.

"If man not pleased, make go hungry," Anya replied.

"They do that in your village?"

"Sometime Father mad and make Anya so hungry Anya faint."

Eli lowered his eyes and thought quietly for a brief time, trying to fathom what life must have been like for her. Then he remembered something critical that he wanted to ask her. He looked up to see Anya looking at him, but she quickly looked away.

Eli asked, "Would you be happy here with me?"

Anya very nearly looked directly at him. "No make Anya go hungry?"

"No, I would never make you go hungry."

"Then Anya like here."

Eli was still unsure of her answer and tried again. "If I were to marry you, would you be happy?"

Anya voice started to quiver, but she seemed more pleading than afraid. "Anya good cook. Anya raise many children."

"But could you love me?"

Anya looked at him, a confused expression on her face. "Anya not understand."

Eli smiled kindly at her. "I would like a wife, but I want her to be able to love me."

Anya spoke hesitantly. "What is love?"

Eli was shocked. No one had ever asked him that before. "What is love! Well, um, love is..."

He paused. How can love be explained? Surely she must know love, but perhaps she didn't understand what the word meant. "Well, it's a feeling you feel in here," he continued, patting his chest. "You feel it when you are around someone who means a lot to you. Surely there is someone you have felt that way about?"

Anya smiled faintly and patted her own chest. "Anya feel good feeling here for Anya's mother."

"Yes, like that. Could you feel that feeling for me?"

"Eli not look like Anya's mother."

Eli smiled. "No, but could you love me, anyway?"

Anya had a look of confusion on her face again. "How woman feel such feeling for man? Anya no need feel. Eli own Anya."

Eli stood, and spoke, trying to keep the frustration from his voice. "No, I don't own Anya." He paused, taking a deep breath, trying to calm his emotions. "I would just want you to be happy here."

"Why not happy?" she asked.

Eli looked into her beautiful, soft brown eyes - eyes that revealed her fear and confusion. He could sense an innocence, and yet, there was a goodness he had never seen in any woman he had ever known. Obviously, he could marry her. Everyone expected that, even Anya. But, he didn't want a wife that was his wife because she thought she was his property. He wanted a wife that loved him and felt she was his equal, as he did; a woman who could bring a strength to their marriage and even feel she had a right to disagree with him.

He had once heard a wise preacher say, "If two people in a marriage never disagree, perhaps only one is needed. For it is in working through our disagreements that we rub off our rough edges and become better. It is not a matter of not having disagreements, but not letting them become rifts that tear apart the very fabric of the marriage." That's what Eli wanted. He wanted a true partner in marriage, not a maid nor a nanny for his children.

He thought of his parents' marriage and what he wanted in his own.

He smiled at Anya to try to ease her concerns and tried another approach. "I mean, would there be any place you would rather be?"

Anya suddenly looked very distant. "Women often talk of place where have much freedom. Place called California, where no man make go hungry."

"If you could go there, would that be what you would rather do?" Eli asked.

Anya turned and looked at Eli with concern. "Eli no want marry Anya?"

"Eli only wants to marry Anya if Anya wants to marry Eli. If you would rather go to California, I would try to send you there. Is that what you would like to do?"

"Anya no thought possible. No thought about."

"You think about it. I'll do what will make you happy. I can send you home or to California."

As Anya considered this, Eli heard someone coming into the room, and he quickly sat on the couch facing Anya. Agnes came in and smiled. "It's good to see you two talking. Dinner's ready."

Eli offered his hand to Anya. She didn't seem to understand. She looked at Agnes. Agnes took Anya's hand and put it in Eli's. He kindly helped her to her feet. Then Agnes took Anya's arm and looped it through Eli's as she had before. The air was filled with trepidation as each glanced furtively at the other, then they hesitantly walked together into the kitchen.

Chapter 5
Jimmy

Eli sat on the dock looking out over the ocean, rolling a piece of driftwood over and over in his hand as he thought. The night was clear and cold, and Eli shivered, not from the cold, but from the emotions he was struggling with. The moon shimmered above the horizon, casting a long sliver of light across the sea, looking like a path leading into the unknown. The water was still, except for a slight lapping along the shore. This path of moonlight looked like a road that he could step onto and walk away on.

But where would the road take him if he walked it? Home? He wondered again where home was. And what was it? Was it with his mother, father, brothers and sisters? Molly was no longer there, at least, not for him. Was that home, or was this his home now; here with Jim? Or was Pennsylvania to be his home? And what about Anya?

The bow of the cattle boat gently nudged against the dock, making a small thudding sound, as if trying to get his attention. He looked over at it. It loomed large in the moonlight. It was as if it had something to tell him, something it wanted him to understand, but it was mute. He would have to find out on his own.

The stillness was broken by the sound of a cane thumping across the dock behind him. He had been so deep in thought he didn't even hear it until it was almost right beside him. He recognized it well and turned to see Jim now by his side.

Jim looked at his young friend, the concern telling in his face and voice. "I thought I just might find you here."

Eli looked up at his old friend and smiled. "I've just been thinking."

"About what?"

"About Anya."

"She's actually a very beautiful girl," Jim said.

"It's more than that, Jim."

Jim nodded. "I saw you glancing at her at dinner. Come to think of it, she glanced some at you, too. I'd say you kind of like her."

"Yes."

Jim grinned. "Then why don't you marry her? You own her, you know."

Eli jumped to his feet and angrily hurled the driftwood out as far as he could into the bay along the moon's silvery path. "I don't own her!" He turned and faced Jim. "A man may control a woman, but he cannot own her heart. He can only have her heart if she wants to give it to him. Her father owned her, but he never had a place in her heart."

Jim spoke in a subdued voice. "I'm sorry. I was only joking."

"This is not a joke!" Eli said. "I am beginning to care for her. But Jim, I only want to marry her if she wants to marry me. I want her to love me."

"Don't you think she will, if you treat her well?" Jim asked.

"I don't know," Eli replied. "I'm not sure she will ever forget the way her father treated her enough to open her heart to me."

Jim sat down on a crate and leaned against his cane. "Perhaps there are more important things than love."

"More important things than love?" Eli asked. "What could be more important than love?"

Eli detected an unfamiliar look on Jim's face. He seemed far away as he answered. "Trust, kindness, gentleness, patience."

"But aren't those what love is built on?" Eli asked.

Jim leaned back so he could look up at his young friend. "When I was your age, I thought so. But I've learned that you can love someone and still not like or trust them very much."

Jim seemed to understand things and know more than he ever told. Eli sat down beside Jim and looked out at the silvery path that was so inviting minutes before, the far distant end blurring as the moon rose higher, illuminating the nearby dock and ship in its yellow strands. The driftwood faded from view, following the moon's vanishing path.

Eli studied his friend. He had always been so dependable. Jim, his hair more silvery than the moonlight on the bay, seemed to be holding something back.

"Jim," Eli asked, "why have you never married?"

Jim didn't answer right away, but he didn't just grunt either. He got up and walked slowly to the edge of the dock and looked down into the bay. The stillness of the evening was thick around them. Nature seemed to hold its breath, as if his secret was its own. His chiseled face shown in the moonlight.

Finally, he looked up, but his mind still seemed far away. "I did."

Eli was shocked. "You did?"

"Many years ago. I had a beautiful wife and wonderful little son."

"What happened?" Eli asked.

Jim's voice began to quiver. "The flu epidemic came through here and took my sweet Mary and my little Jimmy."

Eli could feel his emotions welling up inside of him. In an instant, he understood more about Jim than he had in the whole two years they had been together. "I'm sorry," was all Eli managed to say.

Jim took a deep breath and appeared to be trying to hold his emotions in check. "I guess I always blamed God. I could never remarry. I got so lonely that I thought about taking my own life. That's when you showed up and needed a place to stay." Then, getting back to his old self, he turned and poked Eli with his cane. "And you've caused so much trouble, I forgot all about it."

Eli chuckled, and even Jim managed a smile.

Eli stood up by his old friend and put his arm around his shoulders. "Is that why you have worried so much about Molly coming over?"

Jim turned away. He looked up at the moon and then back down at the sea, but finally spoke. "I was afraid what might happen. Why, I was..." Jim paused. He was not one to show any soft emotion. He regained his composure and turned and prodded Eli with his cane again. "I was just worried I might get stuck with you forever."

Eli snorted. "You old goat. You wouldn't know what to do if you weren't tramping around with me to meetings all of the time."

They stood silently for a moment, then they heard footsteps and turned to see someone approaching. From his silhouette in the moonlight, Eli knew it was Victor, the ship's captain. As he came closer, the sweet smell of pipe smoke floated around them.

The captain looked at them questioningly. "Hello, gentlemen."

"Hello, Captain," Eli and Jim replied.

"Oh, call me Victor," the captain said. "So what bring you men down here this time of night?"

Eli turned and looked out over the silvery bay. "Just thinking. Wondering what to do. Victor, do you believe that God directs our lives?"

Victor took a deep puff on his pipe before answering, and then he looked up at the multitude of stars that sparkled in the sky. "Da." Then he pointed toward the north sky. "Me think God put many thing in life like North star. If we look at them, we be fine. Most men not look, though, and end up on reef."

Eli looked at the north star. He thought about this briefly, then turned back toward the Captain. "Victor, what do you feel is the right thing for me to do?"

Victor shook his head. "Victor no able to answer. God hang different star for each man."

Eli felt so confused. He wished he could know more of Anya's life. He just had to understand. "Victor, what would happen to Anya if we sent her back? Would her father really beat her and sell her again?"

Victor took a puff on his pipe then pulled it from his mouth and blew thoughtfully into the air. "Would definitely beat her. May no sell again."

Eli felt somewhat hopeful. "No? That's what she told me."

Victor looked straight at Eli. "May no sell. May put to death."

Eli felt as if someone had slugged him. "You can't be serious!"

Victor's voice was firm. "Bring dishonor to family if sent back. Perhaps sell again. But perhaps worse. Victor no want take back."

Eli was not ready for this. He looked at the giant ship tapping happily against the dock, as if this was what it had been trying to tell him. His thoughts tore at him. His Quaker and Methodist upbringing questioned how any man anywhere could feel right about such a thing, no matter his religion. How could a human being do this to a fellow human being? How could anyone think that what they felt was dishonor to their family justified taking another person's life, and that God could condone such a heinous act? He questioned the captain further. "Does this happen often where she comes from?"

The captain nodded. "I'm afraid so."

As Eli continued to think about this, he started considering options and other things Anya had said. "Victor, she mentioned California. She said the women dream of running away to California. Do you know more about that?"

Victor tapped his pipe, as he spoke. "Victor knows women often talk of go there. They hear many things, but I not know if true. Often, many things a person hears of place are make-believe and much better than is real."

Eli's voice sounded hopeful. "Could you take her there if she wants to go?"

Victor thought a moment. "Need ticket for boat and ticket for train. Cost fifty dollar."

"Back to fifty dollars again?" Eli asked.

"Much better take there than home," Victor replied.

Eli nodded his agreement. Jim stood up and put his hand on Eli's shoulder. "You aren't really thinking of sending her there, are you?"

"I am planning to do what I think will make her happy," Eli replied.

Victor pulled the pipe from his mouth. "And you pay Gratitude Dowry?"

"I am not going to pay money for someone, as if they are a mere item to be bought or sold," Eli answered.

Victor eyed him narrowly. "Then she not be happy no matter where send her."

"Why not?" Eli asked.

Victor was very somber, but stern. "Because she feel worthless."

Eli slammed his fist down forcefully on a stack of crates. "Somehow I've got to make her understand that the Gratitude Dowry is wrong!"

They stood there for quite some time, the moon rising higher in the sky; each man caught up in his own thoughts. The path across the sea was no longer there; the driftwood had vanished, sailing to some unknown shore. The moon sparkled more and more on things around them. A slight frost was starting to spread across the ridges behind them, and the moonlight across the hills made the landscape look surreal.

The silence was broken by the tap of Jim's cane, as he walked to the edge of the dock and looked thoughtfully down into the bay again. Looking at him standing there, silhouetted against the sea, reminded Eli of the day he had stepped off the ship nearly two years earlier. Jim didn't even turn around as he quietly asked, "If you send her away, what would you do?"

31

Eli walked up beside his old friend. "I don't know. I have no real opportunity for marriage here. All the women are too old or too young. Maybe I was wrong in thinking God brought me here. I guess I would just go on down to Pennsylvania."

Jim turned to look at him. "The town wouldn't be the same. No one would be here to preach, or teach reading and writing."

They stood there for some time, letting the stillnes of the evening wash over them. Finally, Eli patted Jim on the shoulder. "I suppose I better work on my sermon for tomorrow. Good night, Victor."

Victor nodded. "Goodnight, Eli." Then Victor turned to Jim. "Good night, Jim."

Jim looked up for just an instant. "Good night, Victor."

As the captain started to walk slowly back to his ship, Eli turned to Jim. "Coming, Jim?"

Jim forced a weak smile, and his voice was quiet as he answered. "You go ahead. I'll be right along."

Eli started to walk away. He turned back to look at Jim standing by the edge of the dock. He suddenly seemed very old. What was Jim thinking of all of this? Eli made his way back to Jim's cabin, leaving Jim alone.

Jim continued to stand by the edge of the dock for quite some time. He thought of many things. He remembered back to when he was dating Mary. She was so beautiful. He had loved her almost from the minute he met her.

She had worked at the lumber camp helping with food and cleaning. Jim was already foreman at the lumber camp, even though he was only thirty and much younger than many of the other men. Jim could remember the day some of the men started acting inappropriately toward her. She was frightened. He had grabbed a big piece of wood and told them that the first man that bothered her would be wearing a pine bough for a hat. The men knew he meant it, and they never bothered her again. Mary had appreciated his watch over her, and it wasn't long before they became good friends.

Her name wasn't really Mary, but Madileeno, but it was easier for customs to put her down as Mary, and that was what everyone called her. She had immigrated from Italy because of political unrest there. She was the oldest, so her father had sent her ahead to find a place the family could live and have her get a job to help support them when they arrived.

However, things had settled down in Italy, and the family decided to stay there. She had been in Newfoundland for two years when she received word that her family wasn't coming. They requested that she come back home, but she had no money, and they had no means to help her. Besides, by that time, she had fallen in love with Jim.

Jim smiled to himself as he thought about it. At thirty-two, he was quite set in his ways, and, besides, she was twelve years younger. He wasn't sure he wanted to get married. She had told him that if he wasn't going to marry her, she was going to save up to go home. By that time, he couldn't imagine life without her, and he immediately proposed.

He remembered well how much the men teased him.

"You know," a man named Clarkston said, "getting married will make you soft."

"Well, that might be good," Jim could remember saying. "Then some of you might almost be competition when I need to whip you."

Jim had worked hard to get his home ready for his new bride. He added onto the kitchen and put in a new wood cookstove - one of those fancy ones that had a reservoir for heating water built right into it. He patched the roof and increased the size of the living room. He worked on it every night and on weekends, and, by the time they were to be married, he felt pretty good about it.

Jim could remember the wedding vividly. There really wasn't much in the way of a preacher. Sometimes a traveling one might come through in the summer. But, it was springtime and no preacher was available. For that reason, they had John Harris perform the marriage. He was Whitman's father, and the mayor at the time. Most of the men from the lumber camp were there, dressed as well as they could in the clothes they had.

They gathered in the old town hall, which was fairly modern then. Most of the town had turned out for the wedding. It was a big event. He could remember how beautiful Mary was as she came into the hall. He had rented a wedding dress for her from the general store, probably the only such dress in town, but her beautiful black hair streaming down her back and her dark brown eyes shining out from under the veil made him catch his breath.

He was so happy to be married to her. He didn't know, however, until after they were married, how much she had to sacrifice. He hadn't known her father had told her that if she married someone outside their faith, and who was not Italian, he would disown her. He hadn't known because she didn't tell him. But about six months after they were married, he came home to find her crying. The open letter by her side told him something was wrong with her family, but he couldn't read at all, nor could he understand Italian.

At first, she wouldn't tell him what the letter said, but he had finally coaxed it out of her. It made him angry - not at her, but at her family. But, as time went on, he began to understand them more through her. They had been a close, loving family and they felt as though she had turned against them.

Mary continued to write home, though the letters from home had quit coming. Jim kept encouraging her. Then one day, about five years after they were married, a letter came. It was from her mother. She said Mary's father was softening, and, perhaps, someday, they could see each other again. Mary continued to write, and so did her mother.

Mary and Jim had wanted to have children almost immediately. But children did not come. Not long after they were married, after they talked of having children, Jim had added on another bedroom for a child. After years with no children, the room became storage. Jim was happy and felt quite fulfilled with just Mary, but he knew how much she ached for a child.

They had been married over ten years, and Jim had given up hope of having children, when, one day, he came home, and Mary told him she thought she might be pregnant. He could remember how the excitement built in his heart as time went on.

When the event drew near, the men teased him more. He made anyone and everyone that came to the camp report on how Mary was doing. He had people checking on her every hour of the day while he was at work. He thought the day would never come.

The time finally arrived, and it wasn't day, but night. In the dark of a cool, spring night, he was rushing off to get Agnes, who was, herself, now a young bride and married to Whitman. She was a nurse and a midwife. She and Whitman came right away. Whitman sat drinking tea, while Jim paced back and forth. Whitman was always calm, and Jim could remember how it annoyed him that time.

When he finally heard the baby cry, he could stand it no longer and rushed into the bedroom. Agnes assured him that the mother and baby were fine, and shooed him back out of the room. From then on, Jim, Mary, and little Jimmy spent every free minute together. He would take them fishing with him almost every Saturday. Jimmy could cast his own pole before he was three, and he was baiting his own hook long before that.

He was the cutest little boy, and the men in the camp adored him. Jim always made sure he stayed away from danger, but he had Jim's wit and he would say things that made the men laugh. Jim could remember that day even old grouchy Clarkston was teasing Jimmy. "Now, are you going to grow up and be like Jim? Wouldn't you like to grow up and be like me instead?"

Jimmy didn't miss a beat. "Nah, I will plan to take a bath once in a while." The men roared at that, and old Clarkston just grinned. "Yip. You're going to be like Jim, all right."

It wasn't too long after Jimmy was born that they received their first letter from Mary's father. He told her he loved her and was sorry for how he had acted. He told her he was working to save money so he and Mary's mother could come visit and see her and their grandson, and meet their son-in-law. Each year they had planned to come the very next year, but something would always come up.

Then, when Jimmy was five, the flu epidemic hit, and very few people traveled anywhere. That horrible flu epidemic... It had taken Mary and Jimmy. Jim started to think about that night, but the pain was too great, and he took his cane and slammed it down on the crate next to him.

He hadn't thought about that night for a long time and he wasn't ready to think about it now. He did think about how dark things had been in his life after that. He had become angry and hated even being alive. He worked every minute of the day just so he wouldn't have to go home and face an empty house.

Jim couldn't remember changing, but somehow he knew he had. He found himself getting angry at the men at the camp for the smallest reasons. The men didn't laugh and joke with him anymore. He was well aware of what people thought of him, but his anger against God seemed to boil over against everyone. By the time he retired, he couldn't say that anyone thought of him as their friend.

He thought of how, at his very lowest point, when he didn't even have work to give any value to his life, Eli had come. Eli had changed everything. He had given him hope again. He could remember that day vividly.

On that evening, as he was sitting down to eat, he had looked at the calendar and realized that it was Jimmy's birthday. He had slammed his fork down and walked out the door. The anger had welled up in his heart the further he walked.

He found himself walking down to the dock - to the end farthest out to sea. As he stood there, looking out over the bay, he made up his mind he was going to jump into the frigid water and swim out to where the tide would pull him away from land where there would be no hope of survival.

As he thought back on that night, he realized it had been a beautiful evening - the kind that follows a violent storm. The sun setting in the west painted the sky behind him with beautiful reds and purples. A rainbow, signifying peace and goodness, danced across the sky. He had barely been aware of things around him, as the storm in his heart still raged with terrible fury.

Suddenly, someone was standing by him. It was a young man, who asked him if he knew where he could find a place to stay. Jim remembered continuing to look out to sea, thinking the man would go away. Jim had stood there, ignoring him for a long time. He didn't go away, so Jim finally turned to look at him.

Jim could remember the feeling that gripped his heart as he took in the image of the stranger. He had dark hair and brown eyes, and, for a minute, Jim thought he could see Mary's image in him.

The young man introduced himself as Eli Whittier, and Jim couldn't help but imagine that Eli looked much like Jimmy would have had he been alive on that very day that would have been his thirty-second birthday. Eli seemed to be slightly younger, but Jim thought no one could have looked more like what he had imagined his son would have - at least, what he imagined, when he had dared let his heart think of such things.

He had taken Eli to his own home. Together they ate the meal he had left earlier. Eli had wolfed down the meal like he hadn't eaten in days. Jim was surprised at how much there was. He always only made just enough for himself, yet, with the two of them eating, they both had plenty and there was still some left over. Jim thought the food had especially tasted good that night.

He cleared out Jimmy's room that night and let Eli sleep there. Eli had gone to bed almost immediately, exhausted from his experience and all that his ship had been through. Jim had taken the lamp and peeked into his room. There, with Eli sleeping in Jimmy's bed, he sensed he could hear Mary say, "God let me send you another son. Take good care of him."

Jim had since thought about all the things that had brought Eli to Newfoundland. He wasn't supposed to be there at all, but the lack of work in England, the storm that blew the ship hundreds of miles off course, and many other unbelievable coincidences had all combined, and here he was. Could it possibly be that God did let Mary send him another son?

But what would Eli do if he didn't marry Anya? Would he leave? Jim wondered if he, himself, could go on living if Eli left. He thought a long time about how he had blamed God for the loss of Mary and Jimmy, but the incredible timing of Eli's arrival had to be more than just chance.

He looked up into the heavens at the stars. Had God hung him a star, too; him, an old man, who had turned his back on God? Could there still be a star out there to guide him? Maybe it shone less brightly than the others, but was it still there? Perhaps the star shone brighter when more heed was paid to it. Could God even be looking out for an old man like him?

Jim looked into the sky and did something he hadn't done since he had cursed God after Mary and Jimmy died. He prayed. As he looked at the heavens, his voice trembled.

"Dear God. I know I haven't talked to you since you decided to take my sweet Mary and my little Jimmy. I suppose I blamed you for what happened. You've brought Eli to me, and I thank you. He has been like a son to me. I don't know if you hear the prayers of an old man like me. I know I ain't worthy to ask, but, if you do hear the prayers of this old man, please help Anya to love Eli, so he can stay here. The church needs him, the town needs him..." Jim paused. He looked down, as if ashamed to raise his eyes for what he had done with his life. But he knew that there was no use trying to hide what was in his heart from God. God knew anyway. So he finally admitted, "And, dear God, I need him."

Jim slowly walked home. The stars seemed to sparkle brighter than they ever had, especially one small, dull, blue star. But Jim, deep in thought, didn't notice.

Chapter 6
Church

Eli and Jim always arrived early at the town hall for church. The town hall was used for many things. Before Eli had came to Newfoundland, there hadn't really been any church meetings. But there was no other building in town big enough, so he had received the town council's permission to hold them there.

It was an old log structure. It was solid, even though it had seen better days. It needed some rechinking between the logs and, although the old wood floor inside had become mostly smooth from years of use, some places, where chairs had been set up a lot, had worked up dangerous slivers that would grab the backside of some unsuspecting person that might try to sit on the floor.

It was just one long hallway with a small council room on one end and a kitchen beside it. The kitchen was only used for socials and was well stocked with plates, cups, and utensils, but not much else. It had an old wood cookstove and a big, double sink. Eli wondered about this kitchen. In the two years he had been there, he had never seen any kind of town social.

In the main hall, folding chairs were stacked along the wall. These had to be set up for church meetings and other events. There was a small pot-bellied stove which had a voracious appetite for wood and still only warmed a small area near it. It was at the end of the long hall near the council rooms. There was a big fireplace along the one long wall, but it was used more for a cheery fire and not truly for heat.

Eli could still remember the resistance he faced trying to have church meetings on Sunday. Even though Jim eventually helped him get the city council and Whitman, as mayor, to let them use the building, it had been Jim that had originally been the most skeptical. He had had a coolness to religion that Eli hadn't understood. But when Jim began to realize how important it was to Eli, he went with him to help convince the city council.

Things had progressed slowly, but surely, from that small, first congregation of five people. Agnes had brought Whitman, Elizabeth, and Mabel with her. Jim had come along to support Eli. Jim had said he was surprised that Eli was able to get any congregation at all. He said people in those parts weren't all that religious, at least not unless there was some natural disaster.

Eli soon realized that an important part of religion is the ability to read. With the exception of Jim, those few who came to church all knew how. He started teaching reading and writing in the evening, and there was a large group that came. But the number of people in his class was seasonal and sporadic - more in the winter than during the rest of the year. Those who did come made a lot of progress and most of them also began coming to church.

Eli thought about his own religious upbringing. His father was Methodist, and his mother was Quaker. Between the two, he had been trained to do a small amount of preaching and had been taught to do what he could to help those around him. But he didn't plan to become the town preacher and didn't think of himself that way, even though everyone else did. He didn't have any real training other than as a lay member.

Some of the men grumbled that he stirred up trouble since their wives now made them come to church, but Eli could sense they didn't really hold any animosity toward him. He was sure they mostly did it to act tough.

It was Whitman who first suggested the town hall ought to have a church bell. "If it is going to be used for learning and church, it ought to look more like one."

Eli, with help from Whitman and Jim, had organized men to build a small steeple on the front of the building near the door. It would double as the bell tower. The town council didn't want to spend money on a bell, so it all had to be raised through donations. They had held a baked food sale that had earned them enough for the down payment, so it could be ordered, and Friday was to be a big social that would hopefully finish earning the rest of the money that was needed.

For the church and school, Eli had been able to come up with an old bookshelf donated by Mr. Klampton, left over from remodeling his general store. Eli put a few books on it, available to anyone who was interested, and that was the extent of the town library. Most of the books were his own - books he had brought from home - but a few people donated some to help in his school efforts. Each week he carried to church his prized possession, his Bible.

The day after Anya came, Eli and Jim arrived at the church early as usual, and Eli built a fire and then swept while Jim was busy setting up chairs. Jim was always there to help. He was very strong for an old man, and Eli wondered if Jim ever really needed the cane for anything besides intimidating anyone who got in his road. He didn't seem to have too much trouble putting his cane aside when he wanted to.

They set the chairs up in ever widening semicircles facing the stove. The podium was near the heat, and it made Eli sweat when he preached. He found himself already sweating today from apprehension, even before the fire was lit. He had hardly slept all night. He had written many sermons, only to throw them away. He knew only a part of what the town was thinking about the situation, but he knew they were expecting some news this Sunday.

Thanks to Jim's help, they were just finishing the preparations when the first people started to arrive. Many came a good fifteen minutes earlier than usual, apparently afraid they wouldn't get good seats for what they thought was obviously going to be a classic sermon.

Eli went to the door to greet everyone as they entered. Mabel and Elizabeth were the first to arrive. They each pulled their unwilling husbands to the front row, being careful to leave the seat Jim always sat in. They also reserved three extra seats; the two that Whitman and Agnes always sat in, and an extra for Anya.

The hall was filling up, and Eli had to enlist a few men to help set up extra chairs, as he called out to those still arriving, "There are still plenty of seats, folks. Come on in. There are even a few up front. I know how much you all love the front seats."

As Jim plopped into his seat, he grumbled. "Folks can't fall asleep up here as easily."

"Yes," Mabel said, "and you can hear better, too."

"Yeah," Jim muttered, "there's that disadvantage as well."

When it was almost time for the meeting to start, Agnes made a grand entrance, bringing Anya shyly past everyone. Anya looked scared, and Eli wondered if she felt uncomfortable not having her veil on in public.

As she walked by, some of the men gasped at how beautiful she was, and as they gawked at her, more than one wife poked her husband in the ribs.

Agnes had dressed Anya in a tasteful, modest dress for church - one that matched well with her long black hair, olive skin, and beautiful brown eyes. It was dark blue with a trim waistline and white lace in a "v" down the front and back. There was also a white lace border along the lower fringe of her dress, and the sleeves puffed out just above her elbows.

Eli found himself staring at her again as she took her seat. Even though she seemed to want to remain unnoticed, unnoticed she could not be, and Eli knew it.

He took a deep breath and began. "I have struggled today with what I should preach on. I spent a very sleepless night. I know a lot of you have heard different things about what happened yesterday. I considered just ignoring it, but I realize that it would be best to come right out and let everyone know the truth and put rumors to rest.

"Many of you know that I was waiting for my fiancée. I had come over here without her and was saving money to send to her so she could receive passage. After two long years I had finally earned enough money. Unbeknown to me, she had already married. Not wanting to leave me alone, she sent me a, well, she sent me a..."

Jim stamped his cane on the floor. "Well, she sent you a mail-order bride. Just say it!"

Eli gulped and blushed. "Yes, she sent me a mail-order bride."

The whole room buzzed with chatter, many expressing their disbelief at the rumor that Eli had just confirmed.

Eli continued trying to speak over the din. "The Harrises were kind enough to give her a place to stay while we sort this whole thing out. I want you all to know that I will try to do the right thing in this matter, if I can figure out what that is."

Mabel jumped to her feet. "By all means, you should marry her!"

Elizabeth leaped up facing Mabel. "What if Anya doesn't want to marry him?"

Mabel got right up in Elizabeth's face. "And why wouldn't she want to marry Eli?"

"Perhaps she doesn't love him. Perhaps she even loves someone else. It's so romantic and exciting!"

Mabel sounded exasperated. "Of course she wants to marry him. She came over, didn't she?"

Elizabeth rolled her eyes. "She was forced to come over. I think he should pay the money to send her back."

"And furthermore," Janice Klampton said, rising to her feet, apparently still miffed about the episode down town, "he can send her back and find himself a decent lady from these parts."

From the bench behind the three ladies, Victor rose, towering over Mabel and Elizabeth and even looking down on Mrs. Klampton. "I not take her back. This not good thing," he bellowed.

Even Mrs. Klampton, her bulk barely able to squeeze onto a chair, cowered before him. Elizabeth's voice quivered, but she tried to act brave. "It's not appropriate to take her away from her family."

The captain glared down at her. "You not know what you talk about."

Mabel jumped back into the conversation, buoyed by what the captain was saying. "I still think he should marry her. She won't want to go back on a cattle boat."

Jim rose and stamped his cane on the floor. "I think you should all be quiet and let Eli speak."

Elizabeth rolled her eyes. "You men are all the same, thinking you can tell us women what to do."

Jim's eyes sparked with fire and his voice with disgust. He pointed his cane menacingly at Elizabeth. "Now, wait a minute. Must I remind you that it was his fiancée, Dolly..."

" Molly," Eli said, interrupting.

Jim started again, hardly missing a beat. "It was his fiancée Molly who sent Anya here, and she's a female!"

Elizabeth gave a disgusted grunt. "I bet her husband put her up to it." Janice nodded, scowling at Jim.

By this time, everyone was starting to voice their opinions. Eli felt he had better try to get the meeting back to order. "Now, calm down, all of you. We are in the church. I'm just trying to set the record straight. I did not come here today to burden the town with my problems. I came here to preach the word of God."

Elizabeth shook her finger at him. "I still think..."

Agnes rose with an air of authority and her voice thundered. "That's enough, all of you! This is a matter for Eli and Anya. You talk as if it's your decision. Well, it's not, and I want to hear the sermon!"

The room went deathly still as everyone looked at Agnes. She was the dominant woman of the town, and when she spoke, the discussion was over. Everyone sank down into their seats.

Eli looked over at Anya. Anya sat there quietly, looking at the floor. No one even asked her what she thought.

He wondered what she did think. She was so far from home, yet he knew he couldn't send her home, not with the fear of her facing possible death. Everyone understood so little, and he knew that, even though he understood more than most, he didn't understand much himself.

Eli nodded to Agnes. "Thank you, Mrs. Harris."

Agnes sat down, but as she did, she shook her finger at him. "But so help me, if you don't do the right thing, Eli Whittier, you'll answer to me!"

Eli blushed as everyone laughed. But he knew Agnes wasn't joking. He took a deep breath, cleared his throat, and started his sermon. "I have chosen for my sermon the topic of love."

Jim burst out laughing. "I can't imagine why."

Eli ignored the comment. "If you had to explain to someone what love is, how would you begin? If they had never felt it or known it, what would you say? In the Bible, there is a story told of Jacob."

Eli came out from behind his podium. He stood right in front of Anya, looking kindly at her. "Jacob went to get himself a wife."

"Wasn't he the one that worked to earn one girl and then the father switched them, so he married the wrong one?" Whitman asked.

Eli gulped. "Well, yes."

Whitman laughed. "Quite apropos I would say."

Everyone burst into laughter, and Eli could feel his face getting warm again. He had preached to these people for two years, worked beside many of them, endured their teasings, and faced challenges with them. He thought how much he loved them, but, right now, he would give anything to have them be like the congregations back home that were quiet and listened without adding their comments. He knew he had no choice but to continue on and get through it.

"Anyway, when he saw the beautiful Rachel, he fell in love with her. For seven years he served her father for her. And the Bible says, 'And Jacob served seven years for Rachel; and they seemed unto him but a few days, for the love he had for her.'"

Jim chuckled. "Well, at least he was there to make sure she didn't marry the postman."

The whole congregation burst into laughter.

Eli looked at his old friend and moved over in front of him. He remembered the day he came off the ship and saw Jim standing at the edge of the dock looking out over the long distances of the sea. He thought of their conversation from the night before. He smiled at Jim and continued. "Sometimes, perhaps we do not know how much we love someone until they are gone. Some of us even wonder if God loves or hears us."

Jim looked up at Eli, then quickly turned away. Eli could see he had hit a soft spot in Jim's heart.

He moved back over toward Anya and looked at her. "The Bible tells us that, 'There is no fear in love; but perfect love casteth out fear.' What kind of fear could there be that would get in the way of love? It could be fear of rejection, the fear of the loss of someone we love, or the fear of abuse by those who should love and protect us the most. If we are to love as God has said, then we must be able to unlock the chains of fear that bind our hearts, and then, and only then, can we truly love another."

Then Eli went right over to Jim and looked him in the eye, as Jim looked up at him. "And true love," Eli said, "will even conquer the fear of loss that extends beyond this life, bringing us together again." Eli paused a moment and then continued the sermon. Eli knew there were things that he could never say that were as important as what he said - things most of the people didn't understand - things that were written only in the hearts of Jim, Anya, and himself. When Eli finished, everyone sat quietly, seeming to sense there was deeper meanings than they understood. For some time he stood silently looking out over the congregation. Quietly Eli said, "Amen," and everyone else murmured their amens in unison.

Everyone was much more subdued as they left. Eli stood at the door to greet them. When Agnes passed, she spoke firmly, but with a bit more tenderness than she had before. "Eli, we expect you and Jim for dinner again tonight."

Eli nodded and said thank you. He looked at Anya as she went out. She managed a quick smile for him. He wondered what she was thinking. Could she ever love him? What would life be like if he did marry her? Could she ever be the independent lady he would want in a wife, or would she always cower around everyone? He met her smile with one of his own, then she quickly turned away.

As the last person filed by and shook Eli's hand, he turned to see Jim alone, still sitting in his seat, deep in thought. He didn't even move as Eli approached him. When he put his hand on Jim's shoulder, Jim jumped. Eli smiled at him. "You're thinking about something, Jim. Care to share it?"

Jim looked away, but not before Eli was sure he saw a glimmer of a tear in his old friend's eye.

"I was thinking about your sermon," Jim said.

"What about my sermon?"

"Your statement 'True love will conquer the fear of loss that extends beyond this life, bringing us together again.'" Jim paused briefly, as if trying to keep his emotions in check, then he asked. "Do you think that my Mary and Jimmy are happy where they are, and that they are somewhere more than just in a hole in the ground?"

Eli paused a moment, trying to put his thoughts into words. "I believe that God has his own timetable for when He takes someone home to live with Him. Yes, I believe they exist somewhere else, and I believe they're happy."

"Sometimes I have felt that I would have been better off to have never married," Jim said.

Eli could feel his own heart wrench in him, as if he was feeling Jim's pain himself. He spoke quietly. "Do you regret what love and time you shared with Mary and Jimmy?"

Jim turned back to Eli, with a look on his face that told Eli he hadn't ever thought about it that way before. "No," he answered.

"Would you be willing to give it up to avoid the sorrow?" Eli asked.

Jim paused, thinking. Finally, he shook his head. "No. It's just that the pain was so dreadful when they died that I thought it would take my very life."

"The greater the love, the greater the sorrow for the loss," Eli said. "But if you believe in God, then you've got to believe in a Heaven, and, if you believe in heaven, you must believe you will see them again, because heaven wouldn't be heaven without those we love."

Jim considered Eli's words for some time. When he spoke, his voice sounded hopeful. "So you do believe we will be together again?"

Eli nodded. "I believe that is the essence of religion, whether you're Quaker, Methodist, Catholic, Jewish, Muslim, or any faith. Our heart just has to find it."

Jim leaned heavily on his cane. "But how do we find it?"

"I don't know," Eli replied. "Victor said that God hangs us each a star in our life to guide us."

Jim agreed and added, "Perhaps we both have watched the wrong stars."

Eli wondered about that. Maybe Jim was right. He knew the star he had been watching in his life was definitely changing. Perhaps it was even the wrong one altogether. He patted Jim on the shoulder. "Well, Agnes invited us to dinner again later this afternoon.

Jim was suddenly his old self again. "One thing about this young lady, we've eaten better since she came. I don't have to put up with any more of your lousy cookin'."

"Hey, I don't cook that badly," Eli said.

"No, but you don't cook that good neither. I ate about half of that stringy roast you had cooking yesterday. Couldn't take no more. It tasted like rawhide."

"I didn't put on a roast. I just put on a bunch of leather straps to soften for the doors of the new cabin I was building for Molly and me."

Jim shook his cane at Eli. "Leather straps? You mean I ate a bunch of leather straps?"

Eli laughed. "The old taste buds aren't what they used to be, eh, Jim?"

"Not since I started eatin' your cookin'. I swear it tasted like one of your roasts, only better. Just needed a little salt, that's all."

Eli laughed. Jim was actually the one that did most of the cooking for them. It gave him something to do to feel important, and he was actually very good at it. Eli wasn't a bad cook and had tried only a few times to help out, but Jim always got annoyed at it and acted like the food was bad.

They started cleaning up and putting the chairs away. As they did, Eli wondered what life was going to bring for both of them, and where their stars would lead.

Chapter 7
Trying To Understand Each Other

Eli was afraid they would be late getting over to Harris's, since Jim took a walk every Sunday afternoon. Jim said it was "...to think about important things," but Eli figured it was more than that. He had once asked if he could join him, but Jim was adamant that he go alone. He was usually gone a long time, but this time he got back plenty early to make it to Harris's before dinner.

They had a wonderful meal. It was a chicken stew. The chicken was in hearty chunks, and the stew was rich and full with lots of potatoes, carrots, celery and a creamy broth. There were thick slices of hot, homemade bread with sweet butter melting into them. Grape juice, a rare commodity in Northshore, was in abundance to drink. For dessert, there was apple pie and ice-cream.

When the meal was over, Jim turned to Agnes. "I'm having a hard time keeping my girlish figure with all these good eats."

Everyone had a good laugh at that except for Anya, and she looked confused. Eli realized that most of what Jim said seemed to go by her.

As they moved to the other room, Agnes grabbed Anya's and Eli's arms, interlinking them, and her sideways glance told Eli that she expected him to start doing more to move the relationship forward.

Jim plopped into a big, soft chair and patted his stomach. "Why, Agnes, that has got to be one of the best meals I have ever eaten in my life."

Agnes smiled and looked directly at Eli. "Actually, Anya cooked this meal."

The surprised shown in Jim's expression. "My goodness, Anya. You are a marvelous cook!"

Anya looked confused. "Mrs. Harris really do most. Very difficult for Anya. Many things different from home."

Whitman seated himself in his usual chair and reached for the paper. Agnes placed her hand on the paper and looked from Whitman to Jim and back. "Where Anya made dinner, I think that maybe Whitman and Jim can help me in the kitchen."

Both men looked at her and knew immediately from the look in her eye that it wasn't a request. Jim struggled his way out of the soft chair and grumbled as he headed to the kitchen, "I hope you've got some of that dish soap that makes your hands soft."

Eli started to follow. "I didn't help cook either. Perhaps I should come help and..."

Agnes turned and blocked his path. She interrupted him, poking him forcibly in the chest. "You, sir, have more important things to do." She pointed at Anya and narrowed her eyes. Eli knew better than to argue. He turned back to Anya as Agnes disappeared into the kitchen.

Eli went to Anya and offered her his arm. She was beginning to understand that custom, and she took it. He led her to the couch, and they sat down, still a good portion of distance between them. They sat there for a brief moment, neither speaking. Eli was trying to think of some way to start the conversation when, to his surprise, Anya spoke first. Her voice was quiet and soft. "Eli ask Anya about Anya's life. Tell Anya about Eli."

Eli was so stunned that it took him a moment to catch his breath, but he finally spoke. "Let's see. I grew up in a small town in Yorkshire, England. My parents were good people who worked hard to provide for our big family. I was the second of ten children. My father worked in a mill and also ran a small acreage. When I met Molly, it wasn't long before we knew we wanted to get married. But times were hard, and there was very little work. We agreed I would come to America and earn enough money to bring her over. It just didn't work that way, I guess."

Eli could feel a tightening in his heart, as the memories of home came flooding back, as well as the overwhelming feelings of loss he had felt when he found out about Molly.

Anya looked at him sadly. "Does Eli miss home?"

"Yes, sometimes I miss home. I miss my father, mother, brothers, and sisters."

Anya looked away. "Anya miss Mother, but no miss Father."

Eli was encouraged that she seemed to be opening up more. "Is it strange to be here?"

Anya nodded. "Anya no understand things here. Sometimes Mrs. Harris say, 'Husband do!', and husband do. No say in Anya's country."

Eli laughed at this. He could just see Agnes saying this and Anya's confusion about it. "Were all men in your country like your father?" he asked.

"Anya think so," she said, "but not know. Woman not speak to man not relative."

They sat there quietly for a moment, then Eli turned to Anya again. "Anya, the captain talked about a custom in your country - that of sending what he called a Gratitude Dowry."

Anya looked at him with worry showing in her face and sounding in her voice. "Eli not worry about Gratitude Dowry. Anya not worth much. Eli no have to pay more than dollar."

Eli realized Anya thought he was concerned about the amount of money. He tried to ease her concern. "No, Anya, I want to know more about it."

Anya lowered her eyes and her voice as she spoke. "Father and husband gather and brag of how much worth are daughter and wife. They say important things."

"So it's important to make your father proud of you?"

Anya turned to look at him. "Not so important Father. More important make Mother happy."

"So it is important to send this Gratitude Dowry to make your mother happy?"

"Mother know if send Gratitude Dowry that daughter worth much and husband treat good. Also, if not good Gratitude Dowry, Father beat Mother."

Eli gasped. He couldn't believe what he was hearing. "You mean if there was no dowry, your father would beat your mother?"

"Father say Mother's fault not give good daughter."

Eli got up and walked a distance away. He couldn't believe what he was hearing. How could this be? His heart was pounding with rage and confusion.

Anya stood, but did not approach him. As she spoke, there was a concern and fear in her voice. "Anya say something bother Eli?"

Eli turned back to face her, unable to keep the emotion from his voice. "Anya, in my home, we never heard of such things. My father loved my mother. He would never consider beating her. He never even raised his voice to her."

A look of disbelief crossed Anya's face. "Mother never do anything wrong?"

Eli laughed, as he thought of his parents. "Oh, my mother did a lot of things wrong. It's just not how things were done. When you love someone, you don't try to hurt them."

Anya looked away, "Anya no understand love."

Eli could sense that his ways and life were as strange to her as hers were to him. He stepped up beside her and reached out to put his arm around her shoulders. Anya barely saw him reach toward her out of the corner of her eye, let out a gasp, and drew away, trembling and cowering.

It was then that Eli realized the depth of her fear. He could feel the swelling in his heart, feelings of love and compassion for her. He spoke quietly. "Anya, I won't hurt you." He carefully reached out and put his arm around her. He could feel her trembling in his arms. "Anya, you're shaking like a leaf."

Anya looked at him, her voice quivering. "Anya frightened. Never have anyone put arm around Anya, but mother."

Eli dropped his arm from around her and took her hand in his. He pulled her to face him. "Anya, remember what I told you about love? The first part of love is trust. You've got to trust that I won't hurt you. You have got to believe that not all men are like your father. Please, Anya."

Her voice still quivered. "Anya try."

They stood there for a brief moment looking into each other's eyes. Eli felt as if Anya was trying to look into his heart and soul, as if she was trying to understand, just as he was trying to understand her.

Just then, Jim, Agnes, and Whitman entered. Agnes smiled to see them holding hands. "It's so good to see the two of you getting to know each other more."

Anya pulled away from Eli. "Anya go bed now."

With that, she turned and quickly departed from the room. Everyone watched her go, then each turned back to Eli questioningly. Eli tried to speak, but, before he could, Agnes glared at him, and her voice boomed accusingly. "What did you do to her?"

Eli's voice was subdued as he spoke. The gamut of emotions he had just been through had left him tired. "I did nothing bad. I only asked her to trust that I would never hurt her." Eli paused a moment, still considering the past few minutes. He knew he still didn't understand Anya totally and he needed to. "Does she talk much of home to you?" he asked.

Whitman dropped into his chair and picked up the paper as he answered. "She won't speak to me much at all. In fact, she tries to avoid me."

Agnes smiled. "She sometimes tells me of her mother. She loves her mother."

"Does she speak much of her father?" Eli asked.

"Just enough that I know he was a very controlling person," Agnes replied. "But I understand that is normal where she came from."

"Do you think she will ever be able to trust men enough to love me?" Eli asked.

Agnes's voice was soft as she seemed to sense what Eli was going through. "That is totally up to you."

Eli didn't know what she meant. He wasn't the one that had caused the problem. Anya's father was. How could she say it was up to him? He queried further. "What do you mean?"

Agnes put her hand on his shoulder, much the way Eli could remember his mother doing. "When a woman feels like Anya feels, the only time she will gain trust in you is when she believes in herself," she said.

"I don't understand."

"I think what she is trying to say," Jim added, "is that Anya's father made her feel like she was nobody. Before she can trust you, she's got to feel like she is somebody to you."

Agnes nodded. "More than that, she has to feel like she is somebody, period."

Whitman looked up from his paper. "But it has to be genuine. Women will sense any falseness in a man."

Everything was quiet for a moment as Eli considered everything that was said. Eventually, Agnes added, "I think you are beginning to care for her."

Eli nodded. "Very much."

"Then, in time, she will know that," Agnes said.

Eli sighed heavily. "Time is something I don't have. The captain leaves one week from today. If she doesn't want to stay by then, I can't force her to, or she will never trust me. And if she doesn't trust me, she can never fully love me."

Agnes nodded. "That is true."

Jim patted his young friend on the shoulder. "Come on, Eli. We should be getting home. Tomorrow is another day, and perhaps things will look brighter."

As they were leaving, Jim turned back to Agnes and grinned. "Thank you for that wonderful dinner. I didn't have to starve to death eating Eli's cooking."

****

After they left, Whitman lowered the paper. "We might as well retire, too."

Agnes smiled at him. "You go ahead. I'll be right along."

Whitman ambled his way off to bed. Agnes went over to the bookcase and took down a picture that was on top. She looked at it carefully and dusted it off. From its depths a young Whitman and a young Agnes stared out at her. He was dressed in a fine dark suit and a top hat from another era that made him look silly. She was in a frilly white wedding gown with a hairdo that would make most people laugh now. She smiled. She could remember how young and happy she was.

Agnes sensed she was not alone. She put the picture back and turned to find Anya standing there. Anya seemed worried, and her voice was quiet as she spoke. "Mrs. Harris?"

"Yes, Anya?"

Anya looked carefully around the room. "Is Mr. Eli gone?"

"Yes, he is. Why, dear? What's the matter?"

"Eli frighten Anya."

"He did? What did he do?"

Anya looked at the floor as she spoke. "Eli say Anya need trust Eli, and Eli put arm around Anya."

Agnes could feel a flood of relief fill her own heart. She smiled at Anya. "Why did that frighten you?"

Anya's voice trembled as she spoke. "Anya feel funny."

"How so?"

Anya put her hand on her own chest. "Anya feel funny here."

"Was it a good feeling?"

Anya stood there thinking for a moment. She raised her eyes to look at Agnes. "Anya not know. Anya never feel before."

Agnes put her arm around Anya. "Does it feel strange for me to put

49

my arm around you?"

Anya smiled. "No. Anya like. Feel like Mother."

"And how does it feel when Eli puts his arm around you?"

Anya paused. She wrinkled her brow. "Feel strange, and... and feel warm, too. Anya scared."

Agnes pulled Anya closer. She felt as if Anya could be her own daughter. Anya leaned her head against Agnes's chest. Agnes could sense Anya was crying slightly. "Anya," Agnes said, "he put his arm around you because he likes you." Agnes reached down and raised Anya's face, so she was looking at her, "Anya, come over here with me." Agnes led her to the book case and pulled the wedding picture down again. "This is a picture of Mr. Harris and me when we were married."

Anya smiled. "Mrs. Harris very beautiful."

"And he was very handsome," Agnes said. "But you know what makes a couple beautiful? It is the love they have for each other. That warm feeling you were feeling was love. You need to concentrate on it and let go of the fear."

"Eli not hurt Anya?"

Agnes shook her head. "No, Eli won't hurt you."

Anya's countenance seemed to relax. "Anya go bed now. Much think about."

Agnes patted her shoulder. "Good night, dear. Sweet dreams."

Agnes watched Anya go off to bed, then looked down at the picture. "I love you, Whitman," she said, then she turned, placed the picture back on the bookcase, and quietly headed off to bed.

Chapter 8
A Long Way From Home

Anya awoke to the sun streaming through her window. Her bed was soft, softer than anything she had ever slept on before. It was completely foreign to her. That first night she had to crawl out of bed and lie down on the floor so she could get some sleep.

It hadn't taken her long to get used to it, however. Within the last couple of days, she had grown to relish the softness of the bed wrapping its down quilts around her. She felt safe and warm.

As she lay there, the warm sunlight streaming over her, she started thinking of home. She would have been up long before the sun called her from her bed - her bed made of grass laid out with a leather mat upon it and another leather hide pulled stiffly over her. Her bed at home never seemed to wrap around her, holding her in its grasp, drawing her into its warmth and security as this one did.

At home she would wake up stiff and sore, shivering from the cold, exhausted at the thought of the long day of work she had ahead of her, even before it started. She would have goats to milk and feed, horse stalls to clean, new rushes to gather to fix the roofs of the house and barns. Their leaking seemed to be one of the great constants of life and drew great wrath upon her from her father. She never could seem to get them right. No matter how well she tried to weave the rushes together, she couldn't get them to hold out the rain.

There was always food to fix, after which her father insisted she and her sisters practice English with an old woman that came to teach them. She never knew why she had to study English, until the day he placed an ad for her in an English magazine.

She could still remember the day her father received the two letters from far away. One had money in it for her purchase and ticket, and the other had a letter she was to take to the man she was being sent to. Her father purchased her a ticket on the cheapest boat he could find, a cattle boat.

Her mother, Katiana, had quietly packed her things, trying hard to be brave. However, when she finished the packing, her stoic manner melted as she handed the bag to Anya. Her mother threw her arms around Anya's neck and sobbed.

Anya even thought she had seen a slight glimmer in her father's eyes as she prepared to board the ship. She, herself, was holding in as much as she could; her father had told her he didn't want a scene. Ivan was highly regarded in the community, but some felt he was making a mistake sending his daughter so far away. He didn't want anything to "fuel their tongue wagging".

The ride on the ship had been without incident. The captain was not excited about delivering her, but he made it clear to his men that she was to be left alone.

She recalled the long voyage. She had a stall, with straw in it for a bed, next to the cows. It was actually more comfortable to sleep on than the bed at home. But the constant swaying made her sick the first week, and she had thrown up more than once. At night it would get cold, and she would leave her bed and lay down next to one of the warm cows that was quietly chewing its cud. She had soon learned which cows were gentle and which ones were not.

There was always plenty to eat, though she quickly tired of pickles and dry bread. The water soon became stale. She came to look forward to the rains, for they would capture fresh water in the rain barrels. She had also found one gentle cow that still had milk and had added that to her diet, which actually made her less homesick. She didn't know if the captain even knew she was milking one of the cows.

Each night, before she went to bed, she would look up at the stars. Her mother had said, "Whenever you feel alone or frightened, look up at the stars and know I am looking at the same stars and praying for you." As Anya would look at the stars at night and kneel to say her own prayers, she would cry and think of her mother. Her mother had always come in to where she and her sisters slept at night. Even when Anya was awake, she would pretend she wasn't, so that she could feel her mother gently pull the stiff covering up. Then her mother would lovingly stroke Anya's face and hair before moving to the next daughter.

It always helped Anya feel loved and secure. But on the ship, there was no one to pull the covering up on her. Her mother had woven her a wool wrap and told her, when she put it around herself, to think of it as if her mother was hugging her.

As the ship labored on, she became horribly bored with nothing to do, day after day. She started cleaning the cow stalls out for a change of pace. The men who were assigned to do the cleaning would try to sneak out of it, which would incur the captain's wrath. So when she started doing it, they were happy and would bring her special treats. Cleaning the stalls made the days pass faster and helped keep her mind off of what lay ahead, even though it reminded her of cleaning the hated horse stables at home.

What lay ahead was what frightened her more than anything. She was sure she must have been sold to a rich man. She had seen how horribly many of the wealthy men would treat their wives. Their wives seemed to be dispensable to them. They could always buy another.

When the captain informed her they would be reaching port the next day, she became frightened to the point she couldn't eat. Until then, she had worked to put it out of her mind, but suddenly, she had to face it. She wondered if her husband-to-be would like her. Would he beat her often? She wondered about the house they would live in and what kind of work she would be doing. How many goats would he have for her to milk? What would his horses be like?

She figured he would have many horses and many goats. Any man that could afford to pay for her what he had paid must surely be wealthy, and he, being wealthy, would have all that went with it. She was sure he would have more than one wife, and she wondered how they would treat her.

She wondered if he would be an old man. She hoped he would be young, but many women in her village were sold to old men. Old men were often richer, able to afford more wives. It made her feel nauseous to think of an old man being her husband knowing that she would be expected to do her duty and provide many children.

The captain had given her some fresh water to clean herself the best she could. She only had one set of clothes, the ones she had on, so she had to wash them while she wore them. She had been concerned she wouldn't make a good impression on her new owner.

The captain had told her to stay on the ship until he could check out the man that she was sent to. The men all agreed. Even though she had hardly said a word to any of them, they all seemed to like her, partially, she was sure, because she cleaned the stalls. One of the men even suggested that, maybe, they wouldn't give her up, and she could stay and work on the ship. The captain wouldn't hear of it. He was a man of honor, and he said he would deliver her, and deliver her he would.

When the captain called for the men to send her down, they all said goodbye. As she started down to the dock, she was trembling so much she could hardly walk. When she reached the dock, she realized there was some confusion, but she wasn't sure what. When the man they called Eli, who was apparently her new owner, had realized she was his, he rushed to her and lifted her veil. The look of shock on his face made her heart flood with fear. Obviously, she was not what he wanted. He must have wanted someone prettier.

Then she delivered the letter that was sent with her. It was supposed to clear things up, but instead, it seemed to cause more confusion. Eli seemed upset and discouraged. She almost felt sorry for him, though she didn't understand why. Then the men all started talking about her. Eli seemed to want to send her back, but the captain refused to take her. What if he sent her back? What would her father do? More than one woman, who had been unacceptable to her new owner, had been publicly beaten or had disappeared, and word was that they had been put to death to preserve the family honor. She was frightened. What could she do to have him accept her?

The decision was made that she would stay a week so they could figure things out. She had one week to try to get him to want her.

When they were finally alone, even though she was afraid to speak in a man's presence, she pleaded with him, wanting him to know she was strong and would bear many children. But that was not what he seemed to want.

He wanted someone to love him. What a strange thing he asked. She did not understand. But last night, as he had put his arm around her, she had felt something she had never felt before. She had felt something like it when he smiled at her - a tingling that ran all over her body. A frightening, but wonderful, sensation she had never known previously. But she had never felt it with so much intensity as she did last night.

He was young and handsome, tall and strong. He did not carry himself as if he were rich, yet, there was a magnificent dignity about him - a strength she didn't understand. He seemed so gentle, yet no one pushed him around.

She found herself drawn to him in ways she didn't dare even think about. Could a man have feelings for a woman, real feelings and not just think of her as property? Is that what his talk of this love was about? There were moments when she would hope for this "love", but she knew she had to keep putting it out of her mind. If she dared think such things, she was bound to slip and say something wrong, kindling his wrath upon her.

Yet he said his own father had never hit his mother. How could that be? Was he making up some strange story? But why would he need to? He owned her and could do with her as he saw fit. Was he trying to impress someone? Perhaps it was that man they called Jim.

Jim was by far the hardest to figure out. He seemed so rough, and yet, at times, he was kind. Was he Eli's father? Eli didn't address him so, and Eli had said his family was far away. Still, Eli often turned to Jim to ask for help, like an uncle or guardian. Jim was an interesting person. This old man, with his gruff ways, still had some kind of goodness about him. When he spoke, she felt she could believe what he said; for good or bad. She knew that Jim spoke things as they were, without any half truths on the edges. She liked that. She liked knowing how things were.

It was Jim who suggested that Eli take time to think about things and not send her home right away. Was Jim trying to help her, or was there more to it? He seemed to want Eli to want her, yet he never commanded Eli that he was to marry her, as a father would at home. At home most men never even knew who their brides were until the night of the wedding. Their fathers arranged things for them.

When Jim looked at her, there was something she couldn't understand. There was a sadness in his eyes, as if he had a hurt that had never healed. She felt compassion for him, and she didn't even know why.

And then there were the women. She didn't know what to make of them. They seemed at times so kind, and yet, at times, so mean. They had taken her and helped her clean. They had her wash and use soap that smelled like the flowers that filled the breeze in the spring time - little soap wrapped in a colorful parchment. When she rubbed it on herself, it helped the dirt come off. They called it soap, but it wasn't anything like the bitter-smelling soap she was used to.

They poured ointments on her hair that, once rinsed out, made it feel like the wool of the angora rabbits. She had never had her hair feel so silky and smooth. When she was all washed, they gave her soft clothes to put on. The clothes were so smooth against her skin that she felt like she had nothing on compared to the rough, heavy, camel-hair garments she was used to. They had her put on all sorts of layers of fluffy white things they called petticoats. A person could see right through them. They had her put on enough layers to clothe two or three women. They had her put a thing on her chest and stomach that had two round cups on it and tightened it until she could hardly breath. They called it a corset. When she mentioned that it was not very comfortable, the one called Elizabeth said, "That's just the way they are, Dearie."

Next, they had her try on all sorts of beautiful clothes. The clothes were soft, light, and smooth to the touch. They didn't reach out and grab her skin and make her itch like her own clothes did. They called these evening gowns, although the one they settled on didn't look like evening at all. Instead it shimmered in the sunlight streaming through the window, reminding her of the sky on the clearest of days. The sleeves were big and round, and they looked like soft, white clouds against the sky.

She put on smooth, sheer stockings, stockings that her legs could be seen through as if she was hardly wearing them at all, and they squeezed her feet into shoes that were higher at the heel than at the front. After watching her stumble and fall over and over, they gave up and traded them for some shoes that were softer and flatter. She couldn't understand why someone would want to wear those other funny shoes, anyway. It would be impossible to work in them.

Next, they trimmed the hair around her face and used a hot thing to curl her hair into rings around her face and collar. When they seemed satisfied with what they had done with her, they stood her in front of a mirror. It showed an image back at her that was much clearer than the stream at home she would gaze into to see herself.

It took her a moment to realize the image was her own. She did not recognize her face without the veil, yet the eyes were the same ones she often saw reflected back at her in the water bucket she had hauled every day. Her hair shimmered and shined, like the manes of the horses after the men prepared them for the parade on Victory Day, and her face was the face of her mother, only younger. She reached up, touching her face and hair, and the hand in the mirror touched the face and hair in the mirror. It really was her. She didn't know for sure, but she thought she might actually be thought of as pretty.

At that moment, the women announced that Eli was there, and it was time to go out where the men were. Her heart had pounded into her throat. Surely, they were not going to take her out in front of men only partially dressed. She tried to tell them she needed her veil, but they didn't seem to understand. The one who was called Mabel said, "You don't have to wear one of those horrible things here. We burned it."

Could it be that they planned to parade her in front of the men as someone would parade an animal? Her neck, face, arms, and even some of her ankles and legs showed. Were they going to humiliate her this way. Then she realized that the other women were dressed similarly. Did women really go around showing their faces, necks, arms, and ankles?

As she entered the parlor, she could not understand the stares on the faces of Mr. Harris and Jim. Again, she thought it was because she was improperly dressed, until she remembered the other women once more. But if this was the way women dressed, why were the men staring at her so?

Then Eli turned around and stared at her. Anya was sure he was going to yell at her for dressing immodestly, but when Eli met her gaze, he only smiled. She tried to smile, but didn't dare allow her eyes to linger, so she looked at the floor, wishing it could swallow her away from this horrible place. She heard Mr. Harris, whom the other men called Whitman, say "She cleans up real nice, doesn't she?"

What could that mean? Eli had stepped toward her, and she feared he might hit her. But as she started to back away, Agnes had grabbed her arm and linked it into Eli's.

Then Agnes ordered the men to leave. Anya felt her body tense at witnessing a woman speaking so boldly, sure one of the men would hit her, but instead, the men got up and started for the kitchen. When Eli started to say something, Jim made it clear Eli was to do what Agnes had said. She couldn't believe that men seemed compelled to comply with the wishes of a woman.

She had felt uneasy when Eli tried to speak to her, but felt if he owned her and wanted her to talk, she should attempt to talk. As time went on, her uneasiness began to subside. He seemed to really want to understand her, and he didn't speak angrily, except once, when she spoke of her treatment at home. Yet his anger was not directed at her, but at the treatment. She knew that, but didn't understand it. Was he angry that he had paid that much money for her and felt she was less than what he had paid for because she had been disciplined so? No man would want a woman that needed lots of correction. Yet, somehow she sensed that was not the reason, but she couldn't comprehend what the reason could be.

Anya's brow wrinkled as she tried to understand. Everything was so different and new to her. She was so confused, far from home, and homesick. She wanted so badly to understand what Eli was saying about love. What she felt he was implying could not possibly be, or could it? Was there a man in the world who thought differently than the men she was used to? Could a man really truly have feelings for a woman, and not just feelings of ownership?

Her thoughts turned to the church meeting. She had gone out in public with her neck, face, and ankles showing. Everyone stared. She realized by then it must not be because of the way she was dressed; all of the women dressed that way. Was it because she was different? Her reflection in the mirror showed that, although her skin was slightly browner, she wasn't that much different. Perhaps it was because she was from outside their village.

She remembered that once in her village, a man had married a woman from another village. All the women had been mean to her. She had even looked like them, but she had been an outsider. Anya wondered if that was the problem here.

But then Eli had started trying to explain something, and everyone started arguing back and forth. Her English wasn't good enough to keep up with them. She did catch that Elizabeth thought he ought to send her back. Was she wrong in thinking that Elizabeth was her friend? She had been so kind just the day before, and now she wanted to send her back; so did another lady. Anya hadn't dared turn around, but she could see the other lady out of the corner of her eye, and she was frighteningly large. That lady seemed to think Eli should marry someone from his own village. Could it be they didn't like her coming into the village and wanted her sent back and possibly killed? This frightened her.

Anya was happy when the captain rose and said he would not take her back. Elizabeth and the big lady seemed frightened of him. The captain was a good man, and she knew he was her friend. Then Mrs. Harris put an end to it all. Anya liked Mrs. Harris. She was kind and protective, and Anya felt safe with her. Anya was glad to have everyone stop talking about her, as if she wasn't even present. The men in her village talked about the women that way, but she had never seen a woman do it. Of course, for that matter, she had never seen a woman speak in a public place with men present.

Then Eli started talking about love again. He seemed to be speaking right to her. He had said that to have true love, you can't have fear. She had thought a lot about that. How could a person not have fear in life? Everything here was so frightening. But the more she thought about it, the more she realized he was not saying you could not have fear, but that you could not fear the person you loved.

She had realized that more last night after he had put his arm around her. She had felt something she had never felt before, or not felt as much. It was like that tingling feeling she got when he smiled at her - a frightening, but exciting feeling. She hadn't meant to pull away, but her whole body quivered with fright - fright that he might strike her, and fear at her own unrecognizable feelings. Mrs. Harris said the feeling was love. Could this be the love that Eli was wanting her to feel? Mrs. Harris said she needed to let go of the fear and concentrate on the good feeling. Was this what Eli meant?

If she could learn to feel this love, maybe Eli would marry her and not send her back. Could he be as good as he seemed? He was young, handsome, and, when she had asked Mrs. Harris how many wives Eli had, Mrs. Harris just laughed. "He doesn't have a wife. That's why you are here." Mrs. Harris had said that no man had more than one wife. Anya had been shocked. Mrs. Harris had laughed again as Anya had asked, "Even if they are rich?"

"Even if they are rich," Mrs. Harris assured her.

Anya mulled this over in her mind some more. What a strange place this was. Men only had one wife, and they wanted their wife to love them.

As Anya lay snugly in her warm bed, the only thing she knew for sure was that she wanted Eli to marry her, and her reasons were beginning to be more than just her fear of going back. As her stomach started grumbling about the late hour, and she knew she needed to get up, she made a resolution to try to let the fear go and believe what her heart seemed to be telling her. Even if it seemed impossible.

Chapter 9
Getting A Man To Want You

By the time Anya came down stairs, she could already hear women's voices coming from the living room. She remembered Agnes had said that Mabel and Elizabeth always came over for tea on Monday. As Anya stepped into the parlor, Mabel was talking.

"Did you hear about that traveling salesman that used the Johnson's outhouse when they were out of toilet paper?"

Elizabeth interrupted, trying to beat her to the punch. "He reached outside and got a handful of stinging nettle."

"You have never seen anybody walk so funny in all your life," Mabel added.

As they were all laughing, Agnes noticed Anya. "Good morning, Anya. Did you sleep well?"

"No, Anya not sleep much."

"Are you feeling ill?" Mabel asked.

"Anya feel fine, but worry upset Eli."

"What could you have done to upset Eli?" Elizabeth asked.

"Anya pull from Eli."

"What?" Mabel and Elizabeth both asked, looking questioningly at Agnes.

Agnes explained about the night before to them, then she turned back to Anya. "It isn't anything to worry about, Anya dear. Eli understands."

Mabel rolled her eyes. "I think it is the best thing she could have done. Why, she wouldn't want him to think he owns her."

Anya felt surprised. "But Eli does own Anya."

Elizabeth stood and put her hand on Anya's shoulder. "Oh, no, he doesn't! You are in Newfoundland now. You are a free woman."

"You can do as you please," Mabel added, also standing up beside her.

Agnes cleared her throat and stood to face the others. "May I remind you ladies that if she doesn't have a husband by Sunday, when the ship pulls out, she will no longer be in Newfoundland. The law says that a person must be a relative of a citizen to stay."

Mabel stuck out her chin defiantly. "One of us could adopt her."

"Adoptions take over a year," Agnes said.

Elizabeth let out a disgusted grunt. "There must be some way. We can't let a man go around thinking he owns someone."

Agnes put her hands on her hips. "Now, where did you get the idea that Eli thinks that?"

Mabel shook her finger at Agnes. "Oh, come, come, Agnes. His money was used to pay for her and send her over here."

Anya nodded. "That why Eli own Anya."

Elizabeth shook her head. "No, no dear. That's what we are trying to tell you. In Newfoundland, no one owns anybody."

Anya felt like she was going to cry. "But Anya want Eli own Anya. Eli nice Anya. Anya think Anya tell Eli, fine put arm around Anya."

Elizabeth grabbed her arm. "Oh, no, no! You can't do that."

"Why? Isn't that what supposed to do?"

Mabel shook her head. "No, no. You don't tell him. You are supposed to hint at it."

"What mean hint?" Anya asked.

"Well, it means...," Elizabeth started to say, but Agnes stepped up and put an arm around Anya lovingly. "It means you should show him you want him to put his arm around you, but you don't really say it."

" How show?" Anya asked.

"You should bat your eyes at him," Mabel said.

Elizabeth shoved Mabel out of the way and grabbed Anya's arm, pulling her away from Mabel and facing herself. "Yes, like this."

Elizabeth batted her eyes at Mabel, like a butterfly caught in a wind storm, while Agnes just rolled her eyes. Both Mabel and Elizabeth had to show her the proper ways for a woman to bat their eyes at a man. Each tried to outdo the other, until Anya thought they looked silly.

"This strange custom," Anya said.

Mabel's face brightened. "And another thing you do is, everywhere he goes, you try to get close to him. Like this."

Mabel snuggled up close to Elizabeth and Elizabeth looked at her sideways, then moved away. Mabel moved up close to her again and grabbed Elizabeth's arm and put it around herself. "See, then he would have to put his arm around you."

Elizabeth spun Mabel out of the way and stepped up to Anya. "But, you can't make him think you are trying to do it deliberately."

Mabel quickly came back over. "Oh, no. You must make him think it's natural."

Anya felt bewildered. "How Anya bat eyes and get close and make Eli think natural?"

Mabel didn't answer her. Instead she tilted her head and put her hands together beside her head. "Another thing you do is blink your eyes gently and stare at him, like he is a happy dream."

"And," Elizabeth added, "when you approach him, you do it when he's not looking, so you are just suddenly there beside him."

Not to be outdone by Elizabeth, Mabel had to add something as well. "And you will also want to make small talk."

"Talk small?" Anya asked.

"No. Small talk," Elizabeth giggled.

"What small talk?" Anya asked.

"Small talk is when you talk about something that is not really important," Agnes explained.

"Like 'How's the weather?' and 'What did you do today?'" Mabel added.

Elizabeth pushed her way past Mabel again. "And 'Do you come here often?' and 'What do you do?'"

The ladies threw out phrase after phrase for Anya to use until her head was swimming. She knew she couldn't remember them all.

"And," Mabel said, as if for a final emphasis to what had already been said, "don't forget to laugh at his jokes."

"Laugh at jokes?" Anya asked.

"Yes," Elizabeth answered, "even if they're not funny."

"How know is joke if not funny?" Anya asked.

Agnes smiled at her. "It's how they say it and what they say."

Anya turned to Agnes. "Anya not understand."

"For example," Elizabeth answered, "they say something that is kind of half off the topic."

Mabel nodded. "Like you might say, 'I went to get my hair fixed today.' Then, a man might say, 'Why, was your rabbit having too many babies?'" Mabel roared with laughter, while the others looked at her blankly as if she was crazy. "You know, hare, rabbit; fixed, have babies," Mabel explained, glaring at them.

Agnes and Elizabeth gave half-hearted, polite laughs while Anya just felt more confused.

"Here, let me give you a better example," Elizabeth said. "You might say, '"I feel like fish tonight. How about you?' to which he might say, 'Well, you don't look like fish, so maybe it's just your perfume.'"

Agnes, Elizabeth, and Mabel all laughed, while Anya tried to smile politely, although she didn't understand what was funny about it.

Anya just shook her head. "So I laugh when man say something strange?"

"No," Elizabeth said, slapping Mabel on the back, "or we'd be laughing all of the time."

Agnes, Elizabeth, and Mabel all laughed again, while Anya just felt even more confused.

"Oh, and don't laugh a deep laugh," Mabel added, imitating a deep, hearty laugh. "No, no, no."

"Just kind of a giggle," Elizabeth interrupted. "It's more feminine."

"Yes, like this," Mabel said, while doing a giggle that half came out her nose in a whistle.

"Not like that," Elizabeth said, interrupting her. "You sound like a cow that's got pneumonia. It's like this."

Elizabeth gurgled a pretend giggle, as everyone stared at her.

"You sound like a seal that swallowed too much sea water," Mabel shot back.

"Oh, yeah?" Elizabeth countered. "Well you–"

"Ladies! Ladies!" Agnes said stepping between them and turning to Anya. "Anyway, Anya, just enjoy being with him."

Mabel and Elizabeth nodded in agreement. They continued on about the finer points of things to do with a man, which they called flirting. They were still talking about it when the door opened. Whitman came in and headed for his favorite chair and the newspaper. The minute he entered, Mabel and Elizabeth changed their demeanor completely and started heading toward the door to leave.

"Now, remember what we told you, Anya," Mabel whispered as she was leaving.

"And just act natural," Elizabeth quietly added, also heading out the door.

Anya turned to Agnes. "How act natural and do *those* things?"

Agnes smiled. "I'm sure I really don't know."

"Weather's warming up just a tad," Whitman said, looking up from the newspaper.

Anya turned and looked at Agnes. "Does Mr. Harris make talk small?"

A confused look crossed Whitman's face as Agnes smiled. "No, he really is talking about the weather."

Anya questioned Whitman. "Eli come over this morning?"

Whitman looked at her in surprise. She was sure it was because she had hardly said a word to him since she arrived. But he smiled kindly at her. "I'm afraid not. He has to work in the woods today. In the evening he usually teaches reading and writing classes."

"When Anya see Eli again?" Anya asked, feeling anxious.

Agnes took her by the arm and led her to the couch. "Would you like to see him?"

"Yes. Anya want do something nice for Eli."

Agnes smiled as they sat down. "That would be a good idea."

"What do you have in mind?" Whitman asked, looking up from his paper.

Anya shook her head. "Anya not know."

"He was really impressed with your cooking the other night," Whitman said. "Maybe you could make him another dinner."

Anya frowned. "Anya not really cook. Mrs. Harris cook."

Whitman turned to look at Agnes. "But I thought you said..."

"Just you never mind," Agnes said interrupting him. "Anya is a good cook. She just doesn't have all the things to cook with the way she did at home."

Whitman dropped the paper onto his lap. "That's it, then. Let's get her the ingredients she needs, and she can cook some exotic dish from her country."

At that, Anya felt excited. "Oh, yes! Anya know just what cook! Most special dinner!"

"That a girl," Agnes said, patting her arm. "I'll help you get what you need at the market. Tell me what it takes, and we'll see what we can do."

Anya started to list the ingredient slowly. "Need pepper, salt, veg-tee-buls..."

"What kind of vegetables?" Agnes asked.

Anya started motioning with her hands. "Green, long, fluffy top."

"Celery?" Agnes asked.

Anya smiled. "Yes, celery. Also need po-ta-to."

"All right," Agnes said.

Anya motioned with her hands again to show the next item. "And red, long, fluffy top."

"Carrots," Whitman said, seemingly proud of himself at figuring out that one.

"Yes, carrots," Anya said excitedly.

"Anything else?" Agnes asked.

Anya thought briefly, then put both hands out in front of her, as if showing a length. "Oh, yes. Almost forgot most important. Need medium size dog."

"Dog!" Whitman and Agnes blurted out together.

"Yes," Anya said, confused at their surprise. "Best meat."

"Anya, dear," Agnes said gently, "I'm afraid it probably wouldn't be a good idea to serve dog."

Whitman grinned. "I don't know. I know one I have been wanting to get rid of."

Agnes turned to him and glared. "Whitman, just stop!"

Anya looked back and forth at the two of them questioningly. "Dog cost much?"

Whitman shook his head. "No. In fact, as mayor, I can tell you where there is a whole kennel of..."

Agnes's voice boomed. "I thought I told you to stop. Don't you need a drink of water, or something?"

Whitman smiled. "Actually, no. This was just getting interesting."

"Whitman!" Agnes's voice made the windows quiver.

"Come to think of it, I was rather thirsty," Whitman said, putting the paper down and retreating to the kitchen.

Anya felt shocked at this exchange, but Agnes just turned kindly back to her. "You see, Anya, there are some differences in our culture. Over here, we don't eat dog meat."

"You no eat dog? What then you eat?"

"Well we eat, chicken and rabbit and beef..."

"Beef?"

"Cow."

Anya gasped. "You eat cow?"

"Yes."

"You eat cow and no eat dog?"

"Yes."

"In Anya's country, eat dog and no eat cow."

Agnes laughed. "Let's compromise. We won't eat cow and you don't eat dog."

"So, what Anya make for Eli?" Anya asked.

"How about a nice batch of cookies?" Agnes replied.

"What are cookies?"

Agnes held her hands in a circle shape. "You know. Little round things you make with flour and sugar."

"What sugar?"

Agnes thought just a minute before answering while Whitman came back in, settled in his chair, and picked up the newspaper.

Agnes started trying to describe sugar. "Well it's sweet, and it's white or brown, and it's..." She paused and turned to Whitman. "Whitman, will you get us a cup of sugar from the kitchen?"

Whitman set the paper down and, with a big sigh, got up and dutifully went back into the kitchen. Agnes turned back to Anya. "I'm sure you'll know it when you see it."

They both waited anxiously for Whitman to come back. Whitman ambled back in, cup in hand, as if he had no care in the world. He handed the cup to Agnes and turned and dropped into his chair again. Agnes held up the cup so Anya could see in it. "Here it is."

Anya looked into the cup. "Oh. Salt."

Agnes shook her head. "No. It's not salt. It's sweet."

"Sweet?" Anya repeated.

Whitman nodded. "Yes. Like, not sour, but sweet."

Anya just shook her head so Agnes held the cup out to her. "Take a little taste."

Anya took the cup, dipped her finger in the sugar, and licked it. It tasted so good. "Anya like!"

Anya put the cup to her mouth and took a whole mouthful. Agnes gasped and reached to stop her, while Whitman looked like he was going to gag.

Agnes pulled the cup away, and Anya could feel a big ring of sugar around her mouth. "Haven't you ever had sugar before?" Agnes asked.

"No! Anya like! Anya want make cookies for Eli!"

Agnes and Whitman both laughed.

Agnes stood up. "Then cookies it is!"

As Whitman turned his attention back to the paper, Agnes led Anya off to the kitchen to do some baking.

As Agnes directed Anya in making cookies, Anya thought about what the women had told her. She had never considered that a woman needed to do things to get a man to like her. In her village, a man owned a woman. She didn't need to get him to like her. She only tried to please him to avoid his wrath.

She thought of things that a woman might do to please a man. She knew her mother tried to cook the things her father liked and to take care of the house so he would not be angry with her. To bat eyes and stare at him seemed ridiculous. If a woman did that at home, a man would think she was ill. It would seem more logical to fix his house, cook his food, and provide him with many children. But Anya was determined to try anything to get Eli to want her.

The more she thought about it, the more she wondered if men also did things to please a woman. In her village, men didn't even try, as far as she knew. Why should they? Once a woman was purchased, what more needed to be done? But Anya could remember once when her father brought her mother a small gift, a pretty necklace, on the anniversary of their wedding. Her father brushed it off and acted as if it was no big deal, but her mother had cherished it. More than once, Anya had seen her pull it from the safety of the little box she kept it in just to admire it.

The more Anya thought about it, the more she knew she did want to please Eli. When Agnes wasn't looking she put in lots of extra sugar to make them better. She loved the sweetness of it. She had never tasted anything like it. It made her mouth dance. She was sure that the more you put in, the better.

But one thing that concerned her about what the women said she should do was that it seemed so insincere. The idea of laughing at someone's joke just to please them, even if you thought it wasn't funny, seemed so fake.

Was a woman supposed to act differently than she truly was to make a man like her? Was she supposed to do that all of her life, or only until they were married? If she was to do something only until she was married, it didn't seem right. It seemed dishonest. Surely a man wouldn't want that. So was a woman supposed to actually change? Could she be someone different than what she was all of her life? She wished that Eli could just like her the way she was.

But as she thought of who she was, her heart sank. She was so different than any of the women around here - different from any woman Eli had ever known. Could she be like them? Did she want to be like them? Could she be happy her whole life, trying to live a lie? Perhaps, if she tried to live like them, she would become like them, and be happy being that way.

65

But how would she know if she was what Eli wanted her to be? What did a man do to show he accepted a woman if he didn't do it by paying for her? Eli had paid for her, even though she understood it was indirectly through Molly, yet he didn't seem to feel he owned her. That really bothered her.

She had always hated the thought of being someone's property, but that was all she had known and with the women here telling her she was free, she felt so insecure. She felt alone and vulnerable. She found herself wanting to belong to someone, even if she was his property. She wanted to know someone would protect her and watch over her, even if he didn't show kindness.

Once or twice she had seen a woman at home cast out by a man, as if she was some stray animal he could dispose of on the street. A woman left to fend for herself very seldom survived very long. If Eli did not want her, what would she do? Where would she go? Would some other man want her?

Then she thought of the feelings she had felt the night before when he put his arm around her. The thought made her tingle inside, and she knew she didn't want just any man. She wanted Eli, and she hoped, somehow, he would want her. If the only way to get him to want her was to do what the ladies suggested, she was willing to try it, even if she thought it was strange.

Chapter 10
Pygmalion

Eli was up early Monday morning, but Jim was up way ahead of him. Even before Eli was dressed, he could smell the bacon sizzling, the aroma of it drifting temptingly into his bedroom. He had gotten up plenty early so he wouldn't be rushed as he tried to plan out his day. As he walked into the kitchen, Jim was working the last of the flap jacks onto a plate.

"You better eat up. I made a lot so you can work faster and get back to see Anya."

Eli grinned as he dropped into a chair. "What are you trying to do, fatten me up?"

Jim shook his spatula at Eli. "Somebody's got to do it. You look like you've hibernated all winter and just emerged from your den looking for a spring meal to kill. Why, if you was working my crew, I'd wonder if you was off your oats, or if we were in the middle of a famine or something."

Eli smiled to himself as he slathered the butter on his pancakes, and it melted, drizzling down the sides. He poured on the rich, brown, maple syrup that cascaded over the layers and across his plate to the crisp brown bacon laying on the edge. Jim had never let him go hungry, that's for sure. He even thought that his pants and shirts were feeling more snug than they used to.

Jim seemed to like to cook. He tried giving Jim a break once in a while, but Jim always complained that something wasn't quite right. Eli came to realize that it wasn't because the food was that bad. Cooking gave Jim something to do and made him feel important. Yet, Eli insisted on taking a turn now and then to make sure he didn't totally lose the skills his mother had taught him.

He was just emptying his plate when Jim dumped a pile of hash browns on it. "Jim," Eli complained, "I'm not going to be able to waddle up to the lumber camp now."

"Aw, sure you can," Jim said. "I ain't given you that much. Besides, you need something to stick to your ribs if you're going to do a decent day's work up there."

Eli barely finished off the hash browns and was careful to guard his plate from Jim. Jim had already packed a lunch for him. There were slabs of buttered bread with slices of elk roast between them, topped with wild onions that grew abundantly in the spring time - one of the few edible things that did.

As Eli headed out the door, Jim called after him. "Hurry right home. I'll have something ready so you can eat and get right over to visit Anya."

It seemed to Eli that everyone in the town was almost more concerned about his matrimonial situation than he was. He started jogging his way to the lumber camp. As the hill got steeper, his breath came shorter. Without this physical work each day, he knew for sure he would have doubled in size, as much as Jim fed him.

Through the day of work, the men harassed him continually about having a mail-order bride. George Andrews, who was by no means Eli's friend if he was anybody's, asked how much Eli had paid for her.

When Eli had told him he hadn't exactly paid for her, George had grinned his semi-toothless grin, "That homely, huh? I guess you get what you pay for."

Eli had wanted to tell him she was beautiful and that a person's value was not summed up in some kind of monetary way, but he thought his breath would just be wasted on George. Though the other men's teasing seemed to be in fun, George's fun, at Eli's expense, seemed ruthless, mean, and coarse.

Eli realized that he was no different than any other victim George tried to humiliate, but George didn't seem to have much sense of decency, especially for things like love, marriage, and intimacy, which Eli felt should be spoken of respectfully and not drug through the mire of common, irreverent language. He found himself trying to avoid being around George and seeking out those who were less harsh. He was glad that no one who had seen her had told George how truly beautiful she was. He was afraid that his anger would boil over if too many disrespectful remarks were made about Anya.

Eli had hoped to get off work early, but ended up working late. As he headed home, Eli shivered as the cool evening air blew off of the bay. He realized he had better get down for dinner before it got too late. He hurried through the meadow full of daffodils and buttercups that glowed slightly in the hues of the evening sun. He quickly bundled some together with other flowers he picked in the forest, and rushed home, choosing his way carefully among the rocks along the face of the ridge.

Jim had dinner ready and was waiting impatiently for him. "Where in blazes have you been? I thought we were going to have an Arctic thaw before you showed up!"

"We had to work late tonight to get the timber quota we needed."

Jim scowled. "If you all just worked faster, you wouldn't have to work longer. Why, when I ran that crew, we worked so hard and fast, we almost never had to work late."

Eli smiled at this. The stories he heard from Jim differed from the ones he heard from those that worked for him. They always said he worked them hard, fast, and late. But he knew there was no use bringing that up.

Eli could smell elk burger cooking, so he hurried and sat down. Jim placed a generous helping of hamburgers with potatoes and gravy in front of him, and his mouth watered. He hadn't even taken a bite before Jim was asking about Anya.

"You are planning to go visit Anya tonight, aren't you?"

68

"Of course," Eli answered, "after I teach my reading and writing class."

Jim let out a disgusted snort and lectured him on priorities, but when they had finished eating, Jim joined him at the town hall to help set up chairs. Jim flopped one chair down and then pointed a finger at Eli, trying to convince him again. "I still think you ought to just forget about teaching tonight, and go over and visit Anya instead."

Eli shook his head. "I thought I would end early, but I didn't want someone to come and not find me here." He paused a minute and looked out the window. "I wonder why no one has come yet."

Jim headed over to get another chair from beside the wall. "With the ice melting and the northern fishing runs opening, maybe everyone has gone fishing."

"I hardly think everyone went fishing."

Jim grabbed Eli's arm and started ushering him to the door. "Well, if no one's here, you ought to just close up and go see Anya."

Eli shook himself free of Jim's grasp. "Would you stop? I'll have plenty of time tonight when I get done."

Jim grabbed his cane from beside the wall and started shaking it at Eli. "That's your problem. You spread yourself too thin. You need to concentrate on getting Anya to marry you and forget everything else. I even think you ought to get somebody to take over logging for you. You wouldn't miss a week's wages."

"Don't think I haven't tried. I talked to my boss, but he wouldn't let me off. He said that, with everyone fishing, he doesn't have enough help."

Jim's face flushed red, and he shook his cane in the air. "I'll talk to him with the backside of a piece of pine, if he..."

Eli grabbed Jim's arm. "Now, calm down, Jim. You remember how scared Anya got last night when I put my arm around her. Perhaps too much time together might not be good."

Jim just grunted. "I know, I know. Absence makes the heart grow fonder. But you know what I think? I think..."

Eli interrupted him, trying to change the subject as he showed Jim the flowers he had brought. "Look. I picked Anya some wild flowers from up along the ridge."

Jim scowled. "Little good they'll do, if they wilt before you can...."

He was interrupted by a knock at the door. Jim looked over at Eli. "Who would be knocking at city hall?"

The door was pushed open, and there stood Anya with Agnes close behind her. Agnes gently pushed Anya into the room as she spoke. "Go on in, Anya dear. You don't have to knock." Then Agnes turned to Eli. "Anya baked you some cookies and wanted to bring them over to you."

Anya was in a nice gingham dress, the kind that women wore for casual wear. She wore a scarf around her hair that had sunflowers across it. Eli thought she was beautiful even if she wasn't dressed up. He smiled as he took the plate of cookies that Anya held out to him. "That's mighty sweet."

Agnes moved up beside Jim. "Well, I really need to be getting home and pick some berries."

Jim shook his head. "But berries aren't on this time of..."

Agnes grabbed Jim's arm and gave him a jerk toward the door. "I'm sure Jim wouldn't mind giving me a hand."

"But I don't want to..." Jim's protesting was interrupted by Agnes whacking him hard on the back.

"Just like Jim, always wanting to help, isn't that right?"

Jim was still gasping for air, but managed to choke out, "that's right," to avoid another whack.

Jim started for the door, herded by Agnes, when Eli stopped him. "Oh, Jim. Wouldn't you like a cookie, before you go?"

As Agnes continued on, Jim turned around. Eli held out the plate of cookies for Jim to take one. Jim smiled as he spoke. "Don't mind if I do."

He took a bite, and suddenly, he looked like he was going to choke. Anya looked pleased with herself. "Anya add lots extra sugar to make 'specially good."

Jim spoke through his gagging. "Yes, I can tell," he gurgled. "They taste like a bowl of molasses. I'll probably have them stuck in my teeth for a month."

Agnes appeared back in the doorway, and everyone knew that was Jim's cue to leave. As Jim stepped out the door, Agnes closed it behind them.

Eli turned to Anya. "It is so nice of you to come over here. I was going to come see you when I got done."

Eli took a bite of cookie and tasted the overwhelming sweetness and suddenly knew what Jim was saying.

Anya grinned at him. "Eli like?"

Eli put the uneaten part of the cookie back on the plate and set the plate on the table. He spoke as even as the sugar bound up his mouth. "I've never tasted anything quite like 'em."

Anya's face showed an embarrassed pride. "Anya first time make cookie."

"Uh, yeah," Eli said, "I can tell."

Anya batted her eyes at him and leaned close. "So how's today?"

Eli backed away. "For what?"

"The weather," Anya said, batting her eyes at him again.

Eli leaned a little further away. "Oh. Oh, the weather. It was fine. Yes a real, real fine day."

"Do come here often?"

Eli nodded. "Yes, I teach here every night."

"What Eli do?"

Eli felt confused. "I, uh, teach here every night."

Anya did an obviously fake giggle. "Eli funny."

Eli laughed politely. "Uh, yeah."

As Anya leaned closer, Eli backed away and then turned to get some chairs. "Anya, I was wondering if you would..."

Eli grabbed a chair and turned as he spoke and crashed right into Anya, who was standing right behind him. "Oh, sorry."

He carried the chair back over by the table and tried to speak again. "Anyway, I was wondering if you would like to..." He turned around, bumping into Anya, who was again right behind him. He leaned back away from her. "Uh, Anya, why do you keep moving?"

"Not supposed to tell."

"What do you mean?"

"Just supposed to hint."

"Supposed to hint what?" Eli asked.

"Ladies say Anya not supposed to tell what Anya want. Only hint."

"Oh," Eli said, beginning to catch on, "the ladies told you this. What did they tell you the hints were?"

"Ladies say Anya to bat eyes," she revealed, batting her eyes at him, "talk small like 'what day is weather', laugh at jokes," she continued, doing her fake giggle, "and move close when Eli not looking," she said, moving up by him.

Eli grinned. "Oh. So that's it. There's only one problem."

Anya looked concerned. "What problem?"

"Sometimes women forget to tell men what these hints are supposed to mean."

"They mean Anya want Eli to put arm around Anya." Then Anya gasped and covered her mouth. "Oh, no. Not supposed to tell."

Eli smiled at her. "That's okay. I won't tell anyone you told me." He took her hand in his. "So it won't scare you if I put my arm around you?"

Anya shook her head. "Anya no more 'fraid. Anya like. Make Anya feel good in here."

She put her hand on her chest. Eli smiled and put his arm carefully around her, and they both blushed slightly. They stood there quietly for a moment, then Eli turned and looked out the window. "I can't figure out why no one else has come tonight."

Anya looked at him innocently. "Oh, Mrs. Harris tell them not come."

Eli turned to look at her. "Mrs. Harris told them not to come?"

Anya nodded. "Yes." Then, pulling herself up to look big and imposing like Agnes, she continued. "Mrs. Harris say no read, write lesson all week. Eli have more important things to do."

Eli grinned at Anya's imitation of Agnes. "Oh, she did, did she?" He paused a moment, realizing that Anya probably didn't have a clue what Agnes was meaning. "Well, I was going to ask you if you wanted to read a book with me anyway, so how about it?"

"How about what?"

"Would you like to read a book together?"

"Anya no read."

"Would you like to learn?"

"Is permitted?"

"What do you mean?"

"In Anya's country, not permitted for woman to read."

"It is here. Here you can learn anything you want. Mrs. Harris, for example, can read very well. Would you like to learn?"

Anya's eyes sparkled with excitement. "Yes! Anya like!"

"All right," Eli said. "Where should we start?"

"Anya look at book?"

"Sure. Come on." Eli took her by the hand and led her over to the small bookcase. "Let's see. Here's one by Shakespeare."

Anya backed away a step. "No like spear."

Eli shook his head. "No. Shakespeare. That's his name."

"Soldier?"

"No," Eli said, "English people just have strange names and... Never mind. It's probably a little too much, anyway. Here's one. *Pygmalion*, by English playwright George Bernard Shaw."

Anya looked confused. "Is about pig?"

Eli smiled. "Oh no. Pygmalion was a mythological Greek sculptor who creates such a beautiful work of art that he wants to marry her. But in this play by George Bernard Shaw, the girl is a flower-girl that is changed into a fine lady presumed to be a princess."

She nodded. "Anya like that story."

"I'll tell you what," Eli said, "let's read some, and then I'll teach you your alphabet."

"Al-pha-bet?" Anya repeated carefully.

"Yes. Those are the letters or symbols that are put together to form words."

Anya nodded enthusiastically. "Is so exciting!"

"Yes, it is. Oh, and speaking of flower-girls. I brought you some flowers."

Eli went to the table, picked up the flowers, and handed them to her.

Anya looked at them as if she was unsure what to do. "Why bring flowers?"

"It's a present. Hasn't anyone ever given you a present before?"

Anya thought a moment. "Sometimes Anya given extra food, if good. We eat flowers?"

She started to take a bite, but Eli stopped her. "No. No. We just look at them and enjoy their beauty and smell them and enjoy their fragrance. Men give them to women they like."

Anya blushed and smelled them. "Umm. Anya like. Anya thank Eli."

Eli smiled. "You're welcome."

He again thought how beautiful she was when she smiled. He led her to a chair by the table and helped her sit down. He sat down beside her and opened the book. Then, he stretched so he could act like he was casually putting his arm around her. She smiled and leaned her head against him as he started to read.

"Preface to *Pygmalion*. A Professor of Phonetics. As will be seen later on, *Pygmalion* needs, not a preface, but a sequel, which I have supplied in its due place. The English have no respect for their language, and will not teach their children to speak it. They spell it so abominably that no man can teach himself what it sounds like. It is impossible for an Englishman to open his mouth, without making some other Englishman despise him. German and Spanish are accessible to foreigners: English is not accessible even to Englishmen...."

They read for a long time. Then Eli started teaching Anya the alphabet. She learned quickly. She was like a dry plant anxious for water. It was almost as if he couldn't teach fast enough; her appetite for learning was insatiable. Eli thought about how, sometimes, when we are deprived of something, it becomes much more valuable to us. Anya had never been allowed to learn and seemed to desire it almost above anything else. Many people in Northshore couldn't read or write, but didn't take the opportunity to learn. Perhaps, because they were not denied the opportunity as she was, it seemed insignificant to them.

By the time they were finishing up for the night, she had memorized all of the vowels and many other letters and could recognize and sound out a few simple words. When it was time to leave for the evening she seemed reluctant to go. She hated to quit learning, but there also seemed to be a yearning in her to be near him. Perhaps he only imagined it because he felt that way about her.

As he started working to put the chairs away, she was right beside him, helping him. She swept as he shut down the fire and closed up the stove. He enjoyed having her work at his side.

He looked at her and, as she worked, she seemed worried. He asked her if there was anything wrong.

"Anya think of girl in story."

"What about her?"

"Anya want understand more. Need explain."

Eli nodded. "Okay, what can I explain?"

Anya frowned as she thought a moment. "Professor Higgins say make flower girl like princess by teach speak better. To make flower girl be princess

73

only need make speak better?"

Eli shook his head. "I'm sure it takes a lot more to be a princess than to just speak properly. I can't really say, since I have never really met a princess. Once, when I was young, I saw the queen from a distance, but I've never really spoken to one or anything."

"Was queen beautiful?" Anya had a look of worry written on her face that Eli didn't understand.

Eli shrugged. "Not really more than any other woman, I guess. I was really small, and I thought my mother was much prettier."

Anya giggled at that, and Eli smiled. Eli wondered about Anya's questions. What was she concerned about? There seemed to be something more behind the questions than she was saying. He wished, for just a brief moment, he could know what she was thinking.

As they stepped into the cool evening air, she linked her arm through his. As he walked her home, he thought to himself that Agnes was training her well.

As he said goodnight, she again seemed reluctant to leave him, which pleased him greatly, for he knew he also felt that way about her. His doubts of whether she could love him began to melt away as the warm sun of hope he was feeling in their relationship started to flow in his heart. He still had concerns about what seemed to be bothering her, but when he turned toward Jim's cabin, the stars overhead sparkled, just like the feeling in his heart did for Anya.

Chapter 11
Could He Approve?

By the time Anya awoke, the sun was streaming fully in her window. She had never slept until after sunup in her life until she came here. She knew it was something she could get used to very easily. However, she didn't want to be lazy. If she was going to be Eli's wife, she wanted to work hard and do well for him. She couldn't imagine anyone having a better husband than she would have, if he did marry her.

But that was what worried her. What if he didn't marry her? What would she do? She was beginning to worry more about Eli not marrying her than about being sent home. She had never imagined a woman could feel about a man like she felt about Eli. When he put his arm around her, the feelings within her would cause a shiver to run up her back and then her chest would get tight and it was hard to breathe.

She remembered how she had once been cleaning stables, when a large stallion came in, rearing and slamming his hooves at her. Her heart had pounded with fright. Her father had driven the stallion away and pulled her to safety.

The feelings she felt, when Eli was near her, was much like that, yet the fear was not there, at least not in the same way. She was struggling to distinguish her feelings. She was experiencing the pounding in her heart and the tightness in her chest, but there was an excitement she couldn't describe. No one had ever talked to her about such things. Was this part of that love that Eli was talking about? Could he possibly be feeling the same kind of emotions for her? She liked how he smiled at her and she noticed that his face would go slightly red when he put his arm around her. She wondered what her own face did.

Could he be experiencing some of the same feelings as she was, or did men not have those kinds of feelings? For that matter, did anyone else have those kinds of feelings, or was she unusual? Oh, how she wished her mother could be there for just a minute. She had wanted to ask Mrs. Harris about it, but she hadn't dared. If Eli found out about her feelings and desires, would he be upset and never marry her?

She thought about the story they had been reading together. It was what Eli called a play. Each of the people in the play would speak, and Eli would try to do their voices. He was really pretty good at doing the different men, but she had giggled to herself when he tried to imitate a woman. As he read, she daydreamed she was Eliza Doolittle. Eliza was a poor girl like herself. Professor Higgins was teaching Eliza to speak properly so she could be a lady. If she were like Eliza, maybe Eli was like Professor Higgins.

This thought brought back the fear that had gripped her heart the last few days. Eli seemed like more than she had ever dreamed possible. Could he possibly want someone like her? She had heard stories of great princes receiving the most beautiful women in the land as a gift - a gift of honor and alliance. But who was she? Though her father was well respected in the community and as well off as any man there, their village was one of the poorest of the poor. She could hardly be thought of as a great gift, and there was no need for an alliance. She was concerned whether Eli even found her to be desirable at all. Was she what a man would consider beautiful, or was she plain?

Was Molly a princess, and was he upset that he didn't get a princess when he paid money for one? She still didn't understand the situation with Molly. All she knew was that Eli said he sent her over two hundred dollars. Her heart sank at the thought of it. Surely, that much money could buy the greatest of princesses.

If he was going to send her away, she just had to know. The uncertainty was worse than knowing a dreaded result. She had planned to ask him last night, but her courage had failed. She had already been bolder than she ever imagined possible. She was driven by the desire to have him marry her. But she had found the courage to do no more than ask about the book and Eliza becoming a princess. She warmed at his comment about his own mother being more beautiful than the queen.

She gained comfort in the fact that, if he did not plan to keep her, he probably wouldn't be teaching her to read and write. Perhaps he was still seeing if she could be the kind of person he wanted. She had always wanted to read and write, but now it meant even more to her. She wanted Eli to see she could do it. She would try hard for him.

She had heard many times, as she grew up, about princesses. She had sometimes thought she would like to be one. They always had fine clothes, lots of food, and didn't have to work hard.

She had heard that the princes actually had so many wives that they didn't even know all of their names. She had always thought that it might also be good to be a princess because a girl could hide among all of the wives, and avoid much of the wrath of her husband. But now, as she thought about Eli being her husband, she wanted him to herself.

As she thought about sharing Eli with another woman, she had another strange feeling come over her. The closest thing to it she could remember was the feeling she had felt when her sister had taken something that belonged to her. It was almost a hatred, but unlike any feeling she had known before.

But this feeling she felt about Eli having another wife was even stronger - much, much stronger. But he wasn't really hers. He didn't belong to her; she belonged to him. Yet she could not clear her heart of this feeling. She couldn't stand it if he had another wife. This feeling was the most intense feeling she had ever felt and she didn't like it, yet there seemed no way to obliterate it from her heart.

She remembered that Agnes said that a man could only have one wife here, and that helped, but she thought, maybe Eli would choose another woman, and then she could never have him. That made the strange feeling hurt her even more.

No one had ever explained about these kind of feelings before. Again she reminded herself, Eli didn't belong to her. And he still hadn't paid the gratitude dowry showing he accepted her. Would she ever really belong to him? No matter how hard she tried to think of something else, that strange feeling kept those nagging doubts at the edge of her mind.

She decided she had better get out of bed and get busy. Being busy would make the time pass faster and help her keep her mind off of those hurtful feelings. Besides, she wanted to study her reading more.

Chapter 12
To Make A Princess

Eli woke with a start. He realized he was already late for work at the lumber camp. He jumped out of bed and hurriedly dressed. The foreman wasn't a patient man. He ran into the kitchen, and Jim already had a lunch for him and some breakfast, too.

"So how did it go last night?" Jim asked.

"Can't talk now," Eli said, grabbing the lunch and some rolls and heading for the door. "I'm late."

"But I didn't get to hear about last night," Jim complained. "And I made a big breakfast."

"Sorry, Jim. You know how the foreman is."

"Well," Jim yelled after Eli, who was now already heading fast for the woods, "just tell him I let you sleep in, and if he has a problem with that, he can take it up with me."

Eli thought about it as he ran. He knew very well the foreman wouldn't take it up with Jim. Eli had learned that when Jim had been the foreman, the current foreman had worked for him. Apparently, Jim had been a tough boss. Some of the men would joke with Eli about living with him. "You're sure going to have your crown in heaven for putting up with an old grouch like him," the foreman had said to Eli.

Eli had chuckled, but he had told them how much he loved Jim and how much he was like a father to him.

"You must have had one rough childhood to think he is like a father," Mr. Jackson had quipped.

Eli smiled as he thought about it. Jim was about as different from his father as a man could be, except for one thing. He knew Jim loved him. He wasn't sure how he knew, but he just knew. Jim had always defended him and stood by him. There was more to it, but he couldn't quite put his finger on it. It was in the way he felt when he was around Jim.

When he got to the camp, the foreman growled at him a little, but, with so many men leaving to go to the fishing runs, he was just glad to have the help. Eli hoped he'd get less teasing today. The men did continue to tease him, asking when the big day would be and when they would get to meet her, but the fun in it was beginning to wear off. As Eli worked, he again avoided George as much as possible. He was afraid that his temper would get the best of him if he had to hear any more of that filthy language.

He thought a lot about Anya as he worked. She was innocent and childlike in so many ways. He felt a desire to protect her, and he knew he was beginning to love her. As he thought of the previous evening, when they had been together, the feelings grew even stronger; it had felt so right. But the concern he had seen in Anya's face and heard in her voice the night before came back to him again. Something was bothering her, and he wasn't sure what it was. He worked hard and kept himself busy to avoid thinking too much about it.

When work was finished, Eli slipped quickly away. The May flowers were starting to bloom on the forest floor. He gathered up a few and added some early spring ferns. He continued up onto Gray Rock Ridge to the meadows. This was one of the places he loved best. He planned to take Anya up there someday, but for now, he kept it to himself.

Although the ridge wasn't that high, it was higher than any of the surrounding area, allowing a clear view of the town and the ocean. In the distance he could make out the rigging on some of the fishing boats as they rocked to and fro gently on the ocean, marching their way back to the bay from a long day out to sea. Eli looked out over the bay. He had worked long hours, and the sun was already descending toward the knoll behind him. The beautiful yellows and oranges flamed their way along the outcropping of rock along the hill. Eli thought of the phrase he often heard Jim say as the evening sky was lit up like a fire from rim to rim. "Red sky at night, sailor's delight." Jim always looked at it as an indicator that the next day would be clear and free of storm.

As he looked at the beautiful sky, Eli sat down to ponder. What would his mother think of Anya? She was so different from his own family. Yet he had a feeling his mother would love her. Anya made no pretense as to who or what she was. She was very honest. In many ways she was like his mother, yet so different.

Eli considered to himself that Anya wasn't like Molly at all. What had made him fall in love with Molly, anyway? Molly was a strong-willed, stubborn woman who enjoyed life. He realized it was her zest for life that made him love her. They went dancing, or fishing, or many different things, and Molly was always in the thick of all of it. She was the life of the party. He felt so alive when he was with her.

Yet, in Anya, he could feel a goodness and kindness, a quiet strength that had not fully been unleashed in her life of unassuming servitude. Perhaps that was what haunted him the most. Could two people of such different backgrounds really intertwine their lives in a gratifying marriage? He realized it was getting late, and he decided he better hurry home.

Jim was impatiently waiting for him. "Where in tarnation have you been?!"

"I just went up on the ridge to pick Anya some wild flowers, and took a minute to sit down and think."

"A minute! Shoot, that's what keeps getting you into trouble. You can't tell time any better than a codfish in a net."

Smelling the strong scent of fish drifting from the kitchen, Eli didn't have to ask what was for dinner. He quickly cleaned up and they sat down to a grand meal of fish, corn bread, honey, and milk.

"You better eat up. I made a double portion today to make up for breakfast," Jim said, loading the table with food. When he finished, he slid into a chair himself and turned his attention more fully to Eli. "So, how did it go last night?"

"Quite well, I guess."

"You guess? You were there, weren't you?"

Eli nodded. "Of course."

"Good," Jim said. "I didn't want to think you snuck off and left her alone or something after I went to the pool hall."

"No," Eli said. "But there seems to be something bothering her."

"Like what?"

Eli pondered for a moment, trying to put the things he had thought of all day into words. "I'm not really sure. She asked me what it took to be a princess and if I had ever met one. I know it is partially because we are reading in a book about a Professor Higgins, who claims he can pass a flower girl off as a princess. But I sense there is more to her question than I understand."

"Well," Jim said, "she's beautiful enough to pass off as a princess - perhaps not an English princess, prancing around in gowns that have enough fabric to clothe a whole town, but a princess from a faraway land."

Eli nodded his agreement. They both ate quietly for a minute, then Eli spoke. "Jim, was it hard for Mary to fit in and get accustomed to things around here?"

Jim paused for a time before answering. When he did answer, his voice was quiet and serious. "You know, Eli, I don't think it was as much a matter of her getting accustomed to things as it was a matter of belonging."

"But isn't belonging and feeling accustomed the same thing?"

Jim shook his head. "You can live in a place all your life, and thus, be accustomed to it, but never feel like you belong. I've seen people born and raised in a community that still feel like outsiders because they have ideas and dreams that don't mesh with those around them."

"Do you feel that, maybe, Anya doesn't feel she belongs?"

"Perhaps."

"So how do you help someone feel at home?"

"I think that when Mary finally felt like she belonged was when she knew I loved her. That might be the problem with Anya. She walks down the street, and people still stare at her; the closest friend she has is Agnes. Until she knows you want her, she will not feel that she belongs here."

Eli sighed heavily. "I am in a tough situation. I may not know if she wants to be here with me until I ask her to marry me, and I really don't want to ask her to marry me until I know she wants to be here with me."

Jim shook his fork at Eli. "You know what your problem is? You do too much thinking. You need to let your heart decide this matter and forget analyzing it. Some questions are better solved by your heart than by your mind."

"That was deep," Eli thought to himself. Sometimes he thought that Jim should have been a philosopher, though Jim didn't even realize how profound he could be.

Eli finished eating and had no sooner gotten the last bite in his mouth than Jim was clearing his plate away. "We better be getting you over to city hall."

They hurried over, afraid Anya might get there before they did. As Eli started building a fire, Jim started setting up chairs. Eli realized he had forgotten to tell Jim about the lack of class attendance the night before. He motioned to him. "Oh, Jim, we won't be needing them tonight. No one is coming."

Jim looked at him, surprised. "How do you know that?"

"Anya said that Agnes made it clear to the town folk that I was too busy to teach this week."

Jim nodded in agreement. "Good for her. So why are we here at all?"

"Anya's coming."

Jim looked shocked. "Anya's coming here? What for?"

"I'm teaching her to read, and we are also reading *Pygmalion* together."

Jim rolled his eyes. "Oh, how romantic," he said sarcastically.

Eli laughed. "We enjoy it."

Jim looked at Eli, the disgust showing in his face. "When I was courting Mary, we used to go up on Gray Rock Ridge, and I can tell you we had better things to do than read a book."

Eli grinned. "Why, Jim. I'm surprised at you!"

Jim shrugged his shoulders, the picture of innocence. "Hey, I was young once. Besides," he grinned slyly, "we just watched the sunset."

Eli laughed. Since Jim had told him of Mary a couple of nights earlier, Eli had wondered why no one in the town had mentioned to him about Jim's family before. Surely, people in the town knew. It was as if everyone held the secret with him. Since Jim had opened up, it was as if the hardened fortress Jim had around him was beginning to crumble. Eli ventured further. "Jim, what was Mary like?"

Jim paused before he spoke. His eyes got a far away look. When he did speak, his voice was soft and gentle with a longing in it. "She had long, dark hair that hung almost to her waist. She would brush it at night, and the candlelight would just glitter off of it. She had big, brown eyes that, when she looked at me, could melt my heart and take any anger away. She was as innocent as a woman could be. I remember one time, she was at the market and a slippery traveling salesman talked her into buying a mop. Why, we didn't have anything but a dirt floor! Oh, at first I was cross, but then she looked at me with those big brown eyes. I figured there warn't nothin' to do but build a floor, so I bought some lumber and put a floor in the cabin so she could use her mop."

They shared a laugh. As Jim spoke about Mary, there was a softness about him that Eli hadn't seen before.

Jim smiled. "It feels good to talk about Mary again. You know, I don't think I have hardly talked about her since she died."

"I like to hear about her. Why haven't you told me about her before?" Eli asked.

Jim looked at the floor. "It was hard bringing back the memory."

It was then that Eli realized why no one had ever told him about Jim's family. It was very likely that any mention of it had, in the past, brought Jim's ire, and people had learned to avoid the subject.

Jim continued. "Now, watching you and Anya, it's as if it were Mary and me. She was an immigrant, too. Scared, not knowing which way to turn."

Eli patted Jim on the shoulder. "I'm glad it's easier now."

"It's more than that," Jim said. "You know how you said something about love and fear?"

"'Love casteth out all fear'," Eli quoted.

Jim nodded. "Yes. That one. It's as if God has brought my life in a full circle, and the fear of being without Mary is gone. I feel I will be with her again."

There was a silence for a time. Eli could feel a love for Jim, like he did for his own father, and, the more he understood him, the more he loved this old man.

The door squeaked open, and Anya, shyly, poked her head in. "Hello. Can Anya come in?"

Eli smiled, went to the door, and took her by the hand to escort her in. "Yes, Anya. You don't have to ask to come into the city hall." He led her over near the warmth of the stove.

Jim grinned at Eli. "I think I probably better be going, but if you ask me, there are still better things to do with your time than read a book."

Eli swatted at Jim in fun. "Get out of here!"

As Jim headed out the door, Anya turned to look at Eli. "What Jim mean?"

Eli's face went red. "Uh, nothin'." Then he tried to change the subject. "So, what would you like to start on tonight? Learn more letters?"

Anya hesitated, and Eli turned to look at her. She seemed unsure of herself, but she had a look of determination and seriousness on her face. "Anya want talk better."

Eli paused, not sure he understood. "Talk better?"

"Yes, like girl in story. Anya want learn talk English better."

"Oh, I see."

"Anya want be lady."

Eli paused, unsure of himself, and wondered if there was more to Anya's request than he was understanding. "Ok. I'm not sure I'm the best teacher for that, but perhaps I can try. Let's see. Let's start with pronouns."

Anya looked at him questioningly. "What pronoun?"

"A pronoun is a word you use instead of a proper name."

"Anya no understand."

Eli led her over to the small table and pulled out her chair. "All right. Let's take that phrase, for instance. Instead of saying 'Anya no understand' you would say 'I don't understand.'"

Anya wrinkled her brow. "'I' mean Anya."

"'I' means the person who is talking."

Anya smiled. "Anya understand."

Eli shook his finger. "Uh, uh, uh."

Anya looked at him shyly. "I understand."

"Good."

Anya took a deep breath and tried some more. "Eli help I speak better."

Eli shook his head as he realized his inadequacy in teaching. She was like a blank slate, and his teaching could affect her for a long time, so he wanted to do it right. He started again. "Let's try some more. You only use 'I' when you do the action. You use 'me' when the action is done to you. So you would say, 'Eli helps me', since Eli does the action, and 'me', because it is Anya getting the help."

Anya nodded. "Oh. Eli helps me."

"Right. Now there are similar words for another person. A person would say, 'You help me', if you speak to the person who is doing the helping. Try a sentence."

"You help me smile," Anya said, looking at Eli and smiling, then turning away shyly.

Eli, not catching what she was saying, continued on. "Good." Then, as it dawned on him what she was meaning, he blushed, but continued. "The word 'you' is used for both the action and the person doing the action, like 'You help me' and 'I help you.' Now, there are mainly just two more sets of pronouns. For a girl you would use 'she' and 'her', and for a boy, you use 'he' and 'him'. For example: 'She smiles at him.' 'He loves her.'"

Eli smiled at her for just a moment. She looked at him, and Eli wondered if his face was as red as Anya's was. Her eyes sparkled as she spoke. "Do you think me ever talk like princess?"

"It would be 'Do you think I would ever talk like a princess?'"

Anya nodded. "Do you think I would ever talk like a princess?"

Eli patted her arm. "That's it."

Anya shook her head. "No. Do you think I would?"

Eli realized she wasn't just practicing. "Oh, you're asking? Yes, I think you will. But it's more important that you feel like a princess."

Anya wrinkled her brow. "How I feel like princess?"

Eli remembered what Agnes had said about Anya needing to feel important. "In order for someone to feel like a princess they must feel good about themselves," he said.

"What mean feel good about themselves?" she asked.

"That means they would have to feel they are worth a lot," he replied.

Anya nodded excitedly. "Like when someone pay much Gratitude Dowry for you?"

Eli looked into her eyes. He could see a yearning which made his heart ache for her. It was as if his heart was trying to teach him what his mind refused to accept, and her heart was trying to send a message to his.

"Is that what would make you feel good about yourself?" he asked.

Anya nodded vigorously. "Yes. Then Anya would ..." She paused, catching herself, then continued. "Then I would know me worth much." She smiled and patted his arm with excitement. "You teach more?"

Her words and their meaning sank deep into his heart. "Perhaps, that is enough on that tonight," he replied. Then, trying to change the subject, he continued. "How about if we read some more in *Pygmalion*?"

Anya smiled. "Anya would like..." She caught herself again. "I would like very much."

Eli retrieved the book from the bookshelf and sat down beside her. As before, when he started to read, she laid her head against his shoulder and he put his arm around her. "Act II. Next day at 11 a.m. Higgins's laboratory in Wimpole Street. It is a room on the first floor, looking on the street, and was meant for the drawing-room. The double doors are in the middle of the back wall; and persons entering find in the corner to their right two tall file cabinets at right angles to one another against the walls. In this corner stands a..."

After reading the book, Eli had her practice some more reading herself. When Eli started working with her on the alphabet, he found out she already knew all of her letters and their sounds. She told him that Agnes had some simple books that she had practiced on with Agnes's help. Eli could see Anya's desire to learn, yet he sensed part of the reason was to please him.

He was surprised at how well she could read. As he praised her progress, she beamed. "You happy I learn read better?"

Eli nodded, and praised her some more. He liked the way her eyes sparkled at his praise. He decided he should start teaching her how to write. He placed a slate in front of them and carefully formed a few letters. He would show her then have her practice. As she concentrated hard on her work, his mind wandered to the gratitude dowry. He felt that if he were to pay it, he would be condoning slavery. But Anya deemed it as a necessary and proper way for a man to show how much he valued a woman. He recalled when she had said she was worth no more than a dollar, and his heart hurt for her at her lack of self-esteem.

His thoughts bounced back and forth. How could he pay it and ever feel good about himself? On the other hand, how could he not pay it, leaving Anya to wonder whether he truly loved her? He would find himself so caught up in his thoughts that he would forget to help her with her letters. Now that he was sure he had figured out what was bothering Anya, his feelings and thoughts were in a quandary.

Anya seemed noticed that he was deep in thought and asked if all was okay. He tried to put her mind at ease by asking her if there was anything she wanted to do the next night. He thought she might get tired of reading and writing all of the time. Her answer made him wish he had never asked.

"Anya want see where Eli work," she said.

Eli was surprised that she would ask to go there. He was leery of taking her to the lumber camp, even though the men wanted to meet her. A lot of young bachelors lived at the camp and didn't come down each night, as he did. The men, for the most part, were good, but their language and lives were coarse and unrefined. It was no place for a lady.

But Eli couldn't let Anya think he was not proud of her, so it was with great trepidation that he agreed. But the more he thought about it, the more nervous he became. He could envision the very worst - the foul language, crude remarks, and cat calls.

They decided to read one more section in the book. He liked feeling her leaning against him. They read until Eli was sure Agnes would be worried about Anya. He put the book away and they cleaned up. It didn't take nearly as long as in the past since they had only needed their two chairs. While he shut down the fire, Anya swept. Though there wasn't much that needed sweeping, it pleased him a lot that she helped so willingly.

When it was time to go, he took the book *Pygmalion* with him, feeling it might hold the key to solving his dilemma. As they stepped into the night, the cold from a light fog bit into them. Eli helped Anya with her coat, then pulled his own on tighter around himself. The fog horn from the distant light house could be heard bellowing its warning across the sea.

Instead of offering his arm, Eli put his arm around her and pulled her close. They walked quietly through the silver mist. Anya snuggled tight against him, and Eli could feel the love he had for her washing away the pain he felt from losing Molly.

After he bid her goodnight, he decided that he had to go someplace to sort things out. Somehow there had to be an answer, he said to himself, as he walked in the serenity of the night.

Chapter 13
What To Do

Eli sat on a crate on the dock, turning the book *Pygmalion* over and over in his hand. The sky overhead was mostly cloudy with a few openings here and there, where the stars twinkled happily. A small breeze was blowing the clouds quietly across the sky. The break in the clouds would open up around the moon now and then, sending a yellow beam down around him, only to close again to cast a much dimmer light across the sky, like a lantern in another room. The clear sky that had shimmered with the earlier sunset, promising a bright new day ahead, had uncharacteristically changed and now warned of a possible storm.

Along the horizon, still free of clouds, the northern lights danced, barely visible along the skyline. They were not all that common or visible in the area, but this particular year they had been brighter and more active than usual. Their patterns of purple and yellow glimmered and danced in swirls along the northern sky rim, like fairies playing in the cool evening air. All of this seemed to pass Eli by as he sat quietly, deep in thought.

Eli's thoughts were broken by the steady, but familiar, tap tap of a cane behind him. He turned to see Jim approaching. Jim didn't say a word until he had plopped himself on a crate beside Eli. "Don't you believe in coming home at night any more?" he asked.

"What time is it?"

"It's almost one in the morning," Jim said. "That would be Wednesday, just in case you have lost track of what day it is, too."

Eli let out a long sigh. "I'm sorry. I didn't realize how long I'd been out here."

"You sure are spending a lot of time here," Jim said.

Eli took a deep breath, inhaling the strong, moisture-filled air blowing off the bay. "It's a nice quiet place to sit and think in the evening. The sound of the waves breaking on the shore is soothing to the soul."

Jim nodded. "So what's troubling you?"

Eli held up the book and pointed to it. "This."

"A book?!"

Eli rose and looked out at the dimly lit sky. " It's not just any book. It's a story of a man who helps a young lady to feel like she's a princess."

"So?"

Eli turned to look at Jim. "You know how I said I would not pay the Gratitude Dowry because it reduces the value of a person and their dignity to the depths of filthy lucre?"

Jim nodded. "Yes, I remember. So what's the problem?"

"Jim, I realize that Anya's feelings of self-worth are tied to how much is paid for her. I thought that if I paid it, I would be accepting the idea of slavery. However, now I realize that if I don't pay it, Anya will always feel she is of no worth to me. I don't feel I can win either way."

"Do you think that was what was bothering her the other night when you were concerned for her feelings about belonging?"

Eli nodded.

Jim thought for a minute, then spoke. "Surely there is some way you can pay it so that her father realizes it is a token of your gratitude and not some kind of slave payment. After all, it is called a *Gratitude* Dowry."

Eli plopped back down on the crate. "But how can I show it is because of my gratitude and not just a purchase acceptance?"

Jim tapped his cane for a moment. He answered as if he was just thinking out loud. "Maybe something out of the norm or unusual."

Eli shook his head. "But, all they seem to understand is money and..." Eli paused and sat there for a moment. Suddenly, he jumped up excitedly. "That's it! That's it!"

Jim looked confused. "What's it?"

Eli patted Jim on the back enthusiastically. "I know what I've got to do. Thanks for the advice. We had better get some sleep. I've got a big day ahead of me."

With that, he headed off for home at a dead run, forgetting all else and leaving Jim sitting on the crate, confused and shaking his head. "Uh, yeah, you're welcome," Jim muttered, as Eli disappeared.

He sat there, pondering what had happened for a moment, when Eli returned. "Hurry, Jim. We've got a big day ahead of us, and I'm going to need your help."

Eli helped Jim to his feet, and together they headed for home, slower this time, while Eli explained his big plans. Eli looked toward the horizon as they walked and talked. He thought the northern lights looked more beautiful than he could ever remember them before. A slight breeze was beginning to blow the clouds away, and the storm that had been building looked like it was going to fade away before it even arrived.

Chapter 14
Hoping He Understands

Before Anya was able to see Eli on Wednesday, Whitman came home carrying some books into the living room where Agnes was helping Anya with her reading. He was thumbing through one of the books. When he spoke, he did so quietly, as if speaking more to himself than to anyone else. "I wonder what has gotten into Eli."

Agnes turned and looked at him. "What do you mean?"

"He's selling all of his books."

Agnes was surprised. "Selling his books? What in the world for?"

"You got me. I asked him, but he wouldn't say. He just said he needed to raise some money."

"But those books are important to him. And he has been using them to teach people to read."

Whitman nodded. "I know all of that. I'm just stating the facts. I'm not saying I have any answers. This morning, before he went to work, I bought a book by Dickens, and this evening I bought a book by Shakespeare."

Agnes looked over at Anya and then back at Whitman, a deep frown creasing her face. "Something strange is going on, and I am going to get to the bottom of it."

Whitman, in his calm, relaxed manner, shook his head, as he realized Agnes's concern for Anya. "Now, calm down, Dear. In the two years we have known that man, he has never done anything mean to anyone. I'm sure he only has the best in mind."

Agnes was on her feet and spoke sternly. "But even the best intentioned person can make a mistake. I mean, he's a man, and sometimes men don't think about everything, especially if it has to do with romance. Some men don't think about it at all."

Whitman kept thumbing through the book for an moment, then stopped as Agnes's last words sunk in, and he realized she was staring at him. "Wait just a minute. I'm a man."

Agnes nodded. "My point exactly."

Whitman let out a little grunt. "I'd just say that some things are a person's own decision, and it is better if others don't interfere." Then, shaking his finger at her he continued. "It is usually those who interfere who make matters worse."

With that, Whitman slipped into the kitchen for a quick bite to eat. It was then that Agnes saw that Anya had a strange expression on her face. "Anya, is something troubling you?"

Anya looked at the floor and spoke quietly. "Mrs. Harris, do you think

Eli like me?"

"I'm sure he does. Why do you ask?"

"He no pay Gratitude Dowry." As Anya spoke, there was an anguish that ripped at Agnes's heart.

Agnes sat down on the couch next to Anya and looked kindly at her. "You need to understand some things about Eli. Eli's mother was a Quaker."

Anya looked up. "Quaker?"

"Yes, a Quaker. A Quaker is someone who believes strongly that things like slavery are wrong. He has had a hard time with the fact that your father sold you to come over here."

Anya took a deep breath, apparently trying to control her emotions. "But I happy here."

Agnes smiled and patted her arm lovingly. "I think Eli knows that. But he has a hard time paying the Gratitude Dowry because he feels he would be condoning slavery."

"But if he no pay, I not welcome ever come home."

Anya nearly choked trying to get the words out and Agnes felt as though her own heart would break. She spoke to Anya encouragingly. "Yes. He knows that. I'm sure Eli is struggling with what to do. I really feel you can trust him."

They sat there quietly for a moment. Anya seemed to be trying hard to regain her emotions. Finally, when she spoke, Agnes could sense it was the real question that was bothering her. She looked directly at Agnes and asked, "Do you think Eli want marry me?"

Agnes smiled and nodded. "Yes, I feel more and more all of the time that he does."

Anya jumped up excited. "I have special present for Eli. I show."

She disappeared into her room. When she returned, she held out the most beautiful jacket that Agnes had ever seen. It had many colors in it that were bright, flowing one into the next, like a rainbow after a hard rain. The blues, greens, reds, and yellows in it were dazzling colors unlike anything Agnes had ever seen before.

Agnes stared at it, unable to believe that Anya could have had such a coat with her when she had been clad so drably when she arrived. "It's beautiful," Agnes said.

Anya held it out for Agnes to feel. It was soft, like the fur of a rabbit. Agnes let her fingers run across it as Anya spoke. "Anya's mother make for Eli. She work many late night when know Anya leave. She hope future husband treat me good, and make present for wedding."

Agnes looked up into Anya's eyes, which seemed to be dancing with excitement. "Anya, do you love Eli?"

Anya looked down and was quiet for a moment. When she looked up her voice quivered. "I no understand, but I feel strange feelings I never feel before. I think this maybe love."

"Yes. I think it is," Agnes said. "Do you want to marry him?"

Anya nodded vigorously. "Yes, very much!"

"Then I think you love him, or are beginning to."

Anya looked at her hopefully. "I hope someday Eli meet Anya's mother."

"Yes, we would all like to meet her," Agnes said. Then, Agnes noticed the sadness come over Anya's face. She put her arm around Anya's shoulders. "Do you miss your mother?"

Anya nodded sadly. "Yes. Very much. I wonder if ever see again."

Agnes gave her a little squeeze. "I'm sure you will get to see her again sometime."

"But not if Eli no pay Gratitude Dowry," Anya said.

"Why not?" Agnes said.

Anya's voice trembled, as if she was going to cry. "Because all in village know I worthless and not accepted."

Agnes pulled Anya close, and Anya leaned her head against Agnes's chest. Agnes patted Anya and stroked her hair. "I'm sure it will all work out. And until it does, you can think of me as your mother."

Anya lifted her tear-glistened eyes and looked into Agnes's face. "I would like very much."

Anya laid her head against Agnes again and cried softly. Agnes continued to stroke Anya's hair. As she did, she spoke quietly, almost to herself. "I hope Eli understands. I sure hope he understands."

Chapter 15
How Can A Person's Worth Be Measured?

As Anya prepared to meet Eli, she thought about the night before. He had become very quiet when she mentioned the Gratitude Dowry. Was he concerned about the cost?

She had come to realize that Eli was not a wealthy man. Although the amount of money that was paid for her was more than twice that of any other woman in her village, he had sent everything he had to Molly; the one who had sent the money to her father.

But, surely, Eli could come up with a dollar. Then she considered that. She wondered what people in her village would think if so much money was paid for her and then only a dollar was paid in the Gratitude Dowry? People would think he was not pleased with her, or was pleased only a dollar's worth.

The women talked about such things. The usual amount that was paid for a woman was set by tradition and varied little. Therefore, the Gratitude Dowry was the one thing that distinguished the value of one woman from another.

She could remember Yolanda, Peoter's wife and the mother of Vladimir Petrovich. All of the girls dreamed of marrying Vladimir. Everyone knew that Peoter had paid a five dollar gratitude dowry for Yolanda. She made sure they didn't forget it, and she lorded it over the other women.

Most women had had two or three dollars paid for them. A few had been valued at four dollars. Her own father had paid three dollars for Katiana, her mother.

But there was one, Maria, whose husband, Taran, had only paid one dollar for her. She was laughed at and derided by the other women. Anya felt sorry for her. She couldn't see that Maria was a worse wife than anyone else, even Yolanda. Nor was Yolanda any better than the others. Yolanda only gave one son and two daughters, and Maria had given her husband eight strong sons and three beautiful daughters. She worked as hard as Yolanda, in fact, much harder. Then how could she be worth only the one dollar that her husband had paid for her? And why did all of the young women dream Vladimir would choose them for a wife? He was no more handsome than Maria's sons. But even she had felt that desire. What was behind those feelings? No one ever really discussed it, but there had to be a reason.

As Anya dressed and thought about Eli, the answer to her question became apparent to her. Peoter treated Yolanda much better because he felt she was of great value. Vladimir would do the same for his wife. He already treated his mother better than Maria's sons treated her. Peoter would not settle on a wife for his son that he thought to be worth less than five dollars;

therefore, Vladimir would treat her that way. That's why Anya had always assumed he would never choose her. She didn't think she could ever be valued at five dollars.

Girls whose mothers were valued at one or two dollars would, likewise, be valued the same by their fathers, and later by their husbands, because that was what everyone expected. Yolanda's mother had also had a husband that paid a five dollar Gratitude Dowry for her. Maria's mother had been valued at one dollar by her husband just as Maria was. And so it went - one demeaning circle - like mother, like daughter.

Anya had assumed she, herself, would be valued at three dollars, because her mother and grandmother were. That was it, then. Value was determined more by what preceded than by anything a person did of themselves. That was the same reason the men in the village tried to breed their horses to the best stallions - so the offspring could sell for more. Just as it was hard for a poorly bred horse to give a valuable offspring, it was also hard for a poorly valued woman to have a highly valued daughter. Value begat value.

So why didn't men try to get a wife that was worth more, and was one woman truly worth more than another, or was it the paying of the higher price that made it seem so? If that was the case, why didn't men just pay more for their wives so they would be worth more? They would more than recoup the value in their daughters. Furthermore, a woman that brought a higher price would feel of more value, and that alone would increase her worth.

And what about the father? Was he not part of his daughter, too? Wouldn't that mean he was no better than the value he felt for his wife? For if he thought his wife was only worth a dollar or two, as well as his daughters, was he not saying that was how he valued himself? Every once in a while, men would pay more for a woman than had been paid for her mother. Then everyone thought highly of her. But also, sadly, sometimes a man would pay less. When that happened, word traveled even faster, and the woman would be avoided and ostracized. Few men would choose to marry her daughters.

Anya wondered about this. Who had determined the value of the first women? Eli seemed to say it was not right for anyone to put a value on another. If that was so, how would a woman know how much she was worth?

Anya thought about the daughters that she hoped to have someday. How much would they feel they were worth? What if Eli only scraped together one dollar? Would that make her daughters of lesser value? The thought ran like a knife through her heart.

Eli had said that what was important was how a woman felt about herself. Could that be the same as the value? Could a person raise her value just by thinking she was worth more? This seemed improbable. Maria couldn't make herself or her daughters more valuable by thinking they were. But could Yolanda make herself worth less?

92

Suppose Yolanda carried herself like Maria, eyes always down, never looking at anyone. The thought made Anya laugh. Yolanda always walked with her nose slightly up, looking down at the other women. There was an old saying: "Pride causeth a man to stumble." She had always thought of Yolanda when she heard this phrase, and thought that a person like her would stumble because she couldn't see obstacles that were right in front of her with her nose in the air.

But it did seem possible that a woman could make her value seem less if she carried herself as Maria did. Those women, whose daughters' gratitude dowry ended up being less, were always women whose husbands chastised them; therefore, they tended to act much like Maria did: eyes turned down, flitting from the presence of others. Their daughters would act similarly. And those few women, whose daughters brought higher gratitude dowries, almost always had husbands who praised them graciously. Could the way a man treated a woman change her value? Didn't the training of a horse make it more or less valuable? Was it any different for a woman - a woman who should be worth so much more than a horse, yet, at times, was treated so much worse?

What could it all mean? If a woman's worth wasn't what she thought of herself, was it what others thought of her? Anya shook this thought off as well. Yolanda might be shocked to know what the other women thought of her and her high-minded ways. But Maria might be surprised as well. Although the women didn't speak kindly to Maria, they still thought well of her. She was always kind and good, though she was humble, timid, and unassuming. Everyone actually loved her. Anya didn't know why the other women treated her so unkindly. Perhaps it was because others did, and everyone was happy to let Maria be the target of the humiliation.

Anya's mind turned again to the value of a woman. If what a woman felt about herself did not reflect what others truly thought of her, and it, likewise, didn't correspond to what she thought of herself, then what could it be?

All of this thinking was almost overwhelming to her. But she needed to make some sense of all of it. Anya remembered that Eli said it is important to feel like a princess. But a woman could only feel like a princess if she was treated that way by others. That must be it, then. A person's worth was not really based on what she thought herself worth, and it was not really what others thought she was worth. It was really the impression she got of herself from others. Yolanda believed everyone thought she was great, though the other women truly didn't. Maria believed the others didn't think she was very important, though in all reality, the women loved her. They each personified the character they thought others viewed them to be. But in time, do not the two - what we think of ourselves, and how we think others view us - become one and the same?

She felt a peacefulness in her heart when she was with Eli - a peacefulness that came from his acceptance of her. She knew that all that mattered to her was what Eli thought of her. She craved his approval. But was what she believed he thought and what he was truly thinking the same? He treated her much better even than Peoter treated Yolanda. Did Eli think she was worth much? He spoke of love, but all she knew was value. When all was said and done, weren't they one and the same? The feelings she had felt over the last days had told her love is something different. But was it totally different? Could she continue to feel those feelings for someone whom she felt did not value her?

That was a question she doubted that she could answer. A question that was tearing at her heart like a ravenous wolf. A question that she was afraid she, too soon, would have to face, especially if Eli refused to pay any gratitude dowry for her.

Chapter 16
The Lumber Camp

Since the moment that Anya had asked to go to the lumber camp, Eli had worried himself sick. It ate at him all day, and by the time he got home from work, he was overcome with his concerns. He had to discuss it with someone, so he finally broached the subject with Jim, even though he knew what Jim's reaction would be.

"Have you plum lost leave of your senses?!" Jim hollered. "You're going to take a nice girl like that to the lumber camp?"

"Well, she asked," Eli said defensively. "Besides, you had Mary up there."

"But, I was there to watch over Mary."

"And I will be there to watch over Anya," Eli countered.

Jim rolled his eyes. "Yeah, right. Like that will do a lot of good."

It wasn't that Eli wasn't tough enough. It was just that Eli knew Jim didn't feel Eli had enough meanness in him. Eli got along with everyone and had never had to defend himself in any of the common lumber camp brawls. But Jim had many times, and from what Eli had heard from the men, he never came out on the losing end.

Jim glared at Eli. "You take that girl up there, and she is likely to forget ever getting back on that boat and heading home, but will just jump in the ocean and swim for it!"

"But Jim," Eli protested, "What could I do? If I refused, she might think I was not proud of her, and she already struggles to believe in herself."

"There is only one thing to do."

"What?"

"I'm going with you," Jim answered.

"But Jim, it's well over two miles."

Jim's eyes sparkled. "If it's too far for you to walk, we can rent a horse for you to ride."

Jim was stubborn, and Eli knew better than to argue him out of it. Besides, Eli had secretly hoped Jim might come along. He figured the men would respect Jim, at least those who had been around a while, and that would add a measure of protection.

Eli left the camp early, and by the time he got home, Jim had packed a picnic they could all enjoy together. They didn't have any time to lose, so they immediately left to pick up Anya. When they knocked on the door, Agnes was waiting for them.

"You're taking Anya to the lumber camp?" she asked, her voice booming with disapproval.

"Well, I..." Eli started to say, but was cut off by Agnes.

"You know very well that is no place for a young woman to be going!"

"Yes, I do, and I was reluctant to, but..."

"Then why the devil are you taking her there?"

Eli was trying to explain it all to Agnes, when Anya came, smiling, into the room. She was dressed in a calico dress with the sunflower scarf across her hair, which hung in a long braid down her back. Her eyes danced with excitement.

"I glad you take me meet your friends!"

Agnes looked at her dolefully. "You're glad?"

"Yes!"

Eli could see this as a good opportunity to explain. "You see, Anya asked me last night to take her up there."

Agnes's eyes narrowed. "Anya asked you?"

Anya nodded happily. "Yes. Mrs. Jackson say is important meet friends."

Agnes looked over at Eli and then back to Anya. "Why?"

Anya seemed surprised. "Why?" Then she leaned close and whispered to Agnes. "Because woman only meet friends if man like woman. I find if Eli want Anya."

Eli was sure Anya didn't mean for him to hear it, but it only confirmed what he already assumed. It apparently also became clear to Agnes. She smiled a beleaguered smile. "You'll take good care of her, won't you?"

"Of course," Jim said, shaking his cane. "That's why I'm coming along."

Agnes had prepared some potato salad and an apple pie. She gave them to Eli to add to the picnic basket. Eli put them in, then reached for Anya's hand. It felt warm and right in his. They started up the road to the lumber camp. It was nothing but a walking path much of the winter, but in the summer it was a well-traveled road. Right now, it was a soggy, furrowed trail, barely beginning to dry out. There was a pronounced, tangy smell from the mint that grew along the streams. At intervals, it would give way to the intense smell of wild onions that were at their zenith in the spring.

They walked quickly, for even though there were still quite a few hours of daylight left, there was also a long way to go. The trees were loaded with blackbirds, and their song created an orchestra that seemed to keep time with the rhythm of their steps. Small sparrows flitted in and out of trees around them, gathering material for their nests. Once in a while, squirrels or chipmunks would dart across the road in front of them.

They had walked quietly for some time, when Jim told them a story about when he was young and how much things had changed in the woods. Eli had heard it before, but it was still good to have a break from the monotony of their journey.

Eventually, the path turned sharply and headed steeply upward in switchbacks along the mountain. Eli could feel a twinge of soreness building in his arm that carried the basket of food. Ordinarily he would have switched the basket to the other hand, but that would mean he would have to switch the hand with which he was holding Anya's.

As they continued to climb, Eli could feel his breath coming harder and harder, and he could hear Jim breathing louder beside him. Even Anya's breathing was more audible, though not much. Eli knew she was used to hard work, and she was obviously in extremely good shape. He could imagine her carrying buckets of water up and down hills to her home.

The road leveled off as they reached the plateau. They paused to catch their breath, and looked back to see the houses of North Shore snuggled in against the mountain, like gingerbread houses in a Brothers Grimm fairy tale. The sea shimmered dark before them as the sun continued its descent to the west.

The road was much easier now, and Eli was glad that it was downhill going home. Although they had covered only about a third of the distance, it was by far the hardest third. They were able to quicken their pace, and it seemed like no time at all before they were reaching the outer parts of the camp.

They were barely within shouting distance, when Eli could hear word being yelled around camp of their approach. They hadn't even reached the first tents when they were surrounded by men. The smell that emanated from the group could have rivaled any pigsty Eli had ever smelled. To make matters worse, George Andrews, with his coarse appearance and attitude, was front and center to meet them. He took one look at Anya and smiled a ruthless, toothless grin. "Hey, Preacher Boy, if you ever think about selling, I'm in the buying mood."

Out of the corner of his eye, Eli saw Anya shrink behind him, and he didn't need to see her face to know the fear that she felt. He could feel it in the trembling of her hand that was still firmly in his. He pulled her farther behind him and faced George.

"I don't own her. She's a human being."

"Well, then," George sneered, "perhaps she would rather have a real man like me."

Eli saw Jim step up, a curl in his lip. "You stay away from her, George."

George spit a wad of chew to the ground. "And who's going to make me? An old man like you?"

Eli's heart began to pound. Had he not only endangered Anya, but also Jim. Jim was an old man, and George was the biggest man in the camp, besides the foreman. He was definitely the meanest. Word was the foreman had whipped him a few times, but no once else had. Eli knew that no one had ever whipped the foreman; that is, no one except Jim, once, in his younger days.

"Leave them alone, George," one of the other men said. Eli realized the others were on his side, and it gave him courage.

George looked around the group of men, wavering slightly. "And which one of you yellow-bellies is going to make me?"

Eli's grip on Anya's hand tightened as hers did on his. "She is with me, George, and we are going to keep it that way."

George started to profane and speak roughly when, suddenly, the foreman was there. "George, don't you have kitchen duty tonight?"

George glared at him. "No, I had it two nights ago."

"Well, you got it again!" the foreman said, getting right up almost nose to nose with him.

George was a big man, but the foreman stood a good four inches taller and was thicker through the chest. Eli still had a hard time believing Jim had ever whipped him. George stood his ground briefly, but finally turned and stalked away.

The whole mood changed immediately, and their coarse language was subdued. Everyone wanted to meet Anya. She shyly came out from behind Eli and smiled at everyone. Eli took some good-natured ribbing as the men joked about "how an ugly guy like him got such a pretty girl." "She ain't got any sisters, does she?" one man asked jokingly.

Anya stood tight against Eli and lowered her eyes timidly. The men followed them, laughing heartily as Eli showed her where he worked. The men were all friendly, but it was a relief for Eli to leave the camp and turn toward home. He was glad that Anya's minimal mastery of the English language did not allow her to grasp all of the colorful language they heard.

They walked briskly back to where the road started down the switchbacks. There, they turned instead, and went a short distance south toward Gray Rock Ridge. Eli set their lunch basket down and laid a thin blanket on the grass. The sun was dipping quickly in the west, and Eli knew they would have just enough time to eat, then they would have to quickly head for home.

Eli suggested that Jim and Anya enjoy the view for a moment while he laid out the picnic. As he pulled out the bread, butter, slabs of roast elk, potato salad, and cold milk, he watched Anya, as she stood looking out over the ocean. Eli again thought how beautiful she was, as the breeze gently tossed the curls around her forehead. He wished he could know what she was thinking. Was she longing for home? Was she still dreaming of California and her thoughts of freedom? Would she be happy here with him? Did their time at the camp help her to know she was important to him, or make her wonder about being with a man like him?

Jim, too, seemed to be in his own world of thought. He was gazing off into the distance, but he was not looking out to sea. Eli turned to see what Jim seemed to be intently studying. He was facing farther south along Gray Rock Ridge. His gaze seemed to be fixed upon a small grove of trees that stood alone on the ridge overlooking the bay. What was going through his mind?

Eli sat silently, watching them longer than he knew he should, but both Anya and Jim seemed so deep in thought. The day was departing quickly, and Eli knew they had to get off of the mountain. The road could be quite treacherous in the dark with its steep drop-offs.

Finally, Anya turned, and he smiled at her. She smiled back, and her smile made his heart light. She joined him on the blanket, and Jim followed. They were all ravenous from the long climb up the road, and they all ate heartily. Eli didn't think he had ever eaten better potato salad, and the elk roast Jim cooked was just perfect, with juice flowing from it as Eli placed the thick slabs on the bread. The milk was still cold and rich with cream.

Eli cut the pie into quarters. He dished out one for each of them. Anya downed hers quickly. Eli liked to watch the delight written on her face when she ate. She really enjoyed her food, and he was sure it was because of the times she had gone hungry. There was one piece left, and Eli offered it to Jim. Jim said he was full, and added, "Why don't you and Anya split it?"

Eli turned to Anya and, when he asked her if she would like more, her eyes nearly danced with excitement. He offered her the whole piece, but she insisted he take half.

When they were finally done, and things were packed, it was dark. Eli was nervous as he turned to Anya. "You will want to stay close because the road has some steep sides."

"The trail is safer," Jim offered.

Eli knew the trail. It went down from the meadow farther south, where he picked flowers for Anya. It was faster and safer, and he took it home often, but Eli was concerned about getting lost.

"I'm not sure we can find it in the dark."

Jim just grunted. "Fiddlesticks!"

He turned and headed toward the meadow, and there was nothing to do but follow. The moon gave a smattering of light, but not enough for Eli to make out the landmarks. Jim marched almost at full speed, and it was all Eli could do to keep up, holding Anya tightly beside him.

As they reached the meadow on the ridge, near the small grove of trees that overlooked the bay, Jim turned sharply, and instantly Eli realized they were on the trail. How did Jim find it? It wasn't a well-marked trail, and Eli was sure it wasn't heavily used. It lead from Gray Rock Ridge but didn't go to any highly populated area. Instead, it wound its way down by Jim's cabin. Eli knew Jim walked this trail every Sunday after dinner. He obviously knew it well.

It wasn't long before they were coming out into the clearing by Jim's cabin. From there, it was a straight path through town to the Harris's home. Jim stayed at the cabin, and Eli walked on with Anya.

Their feet had no sooner hit the porch than Agnes jerked the door open. "Where in blazes have you been?"

"Just go meet Eli's friends," Anya said enthusiastically.

Agnes was prepared for the worst, and Anya's pleasant smile disarmed her. "You know it's almost midnight?"

"Sorry," Eli said. "It all took longer than we expected."

Agnes looked at him questioningly. "And all went well?"

"Basically," Eli replied, deciding not to expound further.

He gave Anya's hand a squeeze and said goodnight. As he walked home, he could still feel what it felt like to have her hand in his, and the memory of her next to him lingered with him. He was sure she was beginning to trust him and care for him. Why else would she have wanted to, as she said, "meet his friends?"

His secret plan burned stronger in his heart, and with each passing day, it was harder and harder to keep from telling her the secret. He was sure he was doing the right thing, and he couldn't wait until Saturday night when he would tell her.

As Eli continued walking briskly toward the cabin, the moon shone brightly and the stars twinkled above; the northern lights shimmered and danced in the northern sky. The whole world seemed to echo his happiness.

Chapter 17
Feeling Secure

Agnes had to hear all about their time at the camp. She pursed her lips tightly as Anya talked about the man with the missing teeth that wanted Eli to sell her. "That would have been George Andrews," she muttered.

Anya told her how Eli kept her behind him, and how Jim had also stepped up to protect her. Agnes nodded approvingly, and laughed when Anya told how the foreman had sent George to work in the kitchen. She smiled as Anya talked about their picnic, the good food, and the beautiful view.

Her brow creased as Anya mentioned the trail off of the mountain. "I wonder where that is. I might have to ask Whitman."

Anya didn't tell her how the men joked about how pretty she was, nor about how they had teased Eli, but she did think a lot about it that night as she lay in her bed wide awake. She didn't like how they had teased him about being ugly. She knew it was just teasing, but she thought Eli was the most handsome man she had ever met. She didn't understand the feeling, but it was almost like she wanted to protect him, too, and she didn't want others saying mean things, even in fun. She tried to put it out of her mind by assuming that men say strange things to each other.

Her mind replayed what the men had said about her. Did men truly think she was pretty? She had always thought her mother was pretty, and she saw the resemblance in the mirror. But could a woman's judgement of a woman's beauty be the same as a man's?

Still, there was something that moved her heart and soul deeper then her concern with being pretty. It was how Eli's eyes sparkled and the richness in his voice when he introduced her to the other men. The sparkle in his eye and the smile he gave her had warmed her heart more than anything she had ever felt. The approval and pride he seemed to feel for her welled up in her and filled her whole being with an excitement that was hard to contain. It moved out to the tips of her fingers and toes and made a tingling feeling shimmer down her back.

She had never felt that approval from her father. She had felt something like it from her mother, but, coming now from a man - from Eli - it was stronger - much, much stronger.

She thought about the peaceful feeling it gave her to have his hand holding hers. She felt calm and secure, even when she was frightened by the man at the lumber camp. She felt Eli was there for her and would protect her. She had shivered, just for a moment, as the mean man had asked to buy her. She had seen women sold in an instant to rich men, but, as she had shrunk back from before the man, Eli had pulled her safely behind him. Although she was scared for Eli, he stood proud and strong and didn't back down to the man, even though the man was much bigger.

Then he told the man that he didn't own her - she was a human being. At first that frightened her, because if he didn't own her, did that mean that someone else would be free to claim her? But he didn't move to relinquish her when the man pressed on, and Eli said she would stay with him. That had made her feel good too.

She was glad when the other man stepped in and the mean man left. But it all still troubled her. Eli said he didn't own her, yet he protected her like she was his and said she would stay with him. Could a woman belong to a man without him owning her? If so, in what way would she belong to him? Standing up against the mean man, he had acted like he owned her. Everything he did indicated he owned her, but what he said didn't.

He had said he wanted her to love him. Her thoughts always came back to that. She wanted to belong to him more than anything else in the world. Could a woman belong to a man in a way other than as his property? It seemed totally implausible, yet that is what everything seemed to indicate.

The more she wondered, the more she confused herself, so she thought about other things. She thought about standing on the edge of the ridge looking out over the ocean. As she had stood there, she remembered the excitement that had overwhelmed her when he had introduced her at the camp. She had never heard her father speak with such pride of her mother. She looked out over the ocean and wished, for one brief moment, that her mother could have the feelings she felt, and she could, in turn, let her mother know what was happening to her. Perhaps, as she continued to learn, she would be able to write to her mother. But still, her mother couldn't read, so it would all have to pass through her father.

She had turned to look at Eli. He had smiled at her, and the feeling flooded over her again. She remembered how he had helped her onto the picnic blanket. She remembered the kind gesture of offering her the last piece of pie. It may not have been a big thing, compared to the many things that had happened the last few days, but it was still unusual to her.

Where she came from, women didn't even eat at the same table as the men. They served until the men had eaten most of the food. Then the women went into another room and ate what was left. Usually, there was not enough, and she was still hungry.

But today she had actually been quite full, yet the pie had been wonderful, and she longed for more. She had insisted they share, and he split it with her. When he handed her her portion - the bigger portion - and smiled at her, it made the pie just that much more delicious.

Then there was the walk down. He had stayed close by her side, his arm around her to keep her from stumbling in the dark. His arm felt so warm and right around her. She found herself pretending to stumble so he would hold her even tighter. She liked the feeling of his strength and protection.

As she finally drifted off to sleep, she thought she would probably never go to the lumber camp again. Agnes had said it wasn't a place a woman should go. But she was glad she had gone this once. She had learned so much about Eli and about herself. It had also given her more things to think about - more questions about herself, Eli, and life here that she could not understand, nor answer, for now.

Chapter 18
Jim

Even with the late night, Eli was up earlier than usual. He decided not to wake Jim, but hurried down to the town center. He set up a little table near the city hall to sell some books. He tried to do this every morning before going to work. He found the early morning hours the best for selling. Those who got up early seemed to have more interest in reading and bettering their minds.

He was able to sell a few books, then he hurried home to prepare for work. Jim was up by then, and breakfast was ready. After a quick bite, he grabbed the lunch Jim had made for him, and he was off.

Eli dreaded going to work that morning. Having taken Anya there, he was afraid what the men would say. The teasing increased briefly, but didn't linger long. George did glare at him more than usual, but even he, soon, seemed to put it behind him. It hadn't turn out as badly as Eli had feared. He thought to himself that, often, our apprehensions of a situation are far worse than the event itself.

Jim had offered to make dinner for the three of them that Thursday evening. Eli asked what the dinner would be, but Jim told him it would be a surprise. Eli laughed at that. He was seeing a change in Jim that made his heart feel good. Jim was smiling and laughing more. He was still ready with his cane to adjust the status quo of things he didn't like, but he was much happier.

Eli hurried home from the lumber camp by way of the meadow to pick some more flowers. He picked extra today. Some were for Anya, and some were for the table. As he followed the trail down, he thought again how Jim always walked this trail and knew it so well.

By the time he got down off the mountain each evening, he was always famished and this night was no different. He was concerned about the time, thinking he might need to help Jim with the last bit of cleaning and preparation. But when he walked into the cabin, it was clean and neat. In addition, the whole house had a tantalizing smell of food like nothing he had ever smelled before.

His mouth watered and his stomach ached. He looked at Jim, who was busy working in the kitchen. "What it that wonderful smell?"

Jim grinned. "You like it?"

"It's grand. I've never smelled anything like it in my life."

"That's because it's Italian. Mary taught me how to make it."

Eli started to lift a lid on one of the pots, but the end of a dish towel reached out like a snake and bit him. He dropped the lid with a clatter. "Ow! That hurt!"

Jim glared at him, but had a twinkle in his eye. "You get yourself cleaned up and get that girl back here, and then you can check it out."

Eli thought, if that wasn't motivation, he didn't know what was. He cleaned up, gave Jim the flowers for the table, and got the others ready for Anya, but he couldn't help but tease Jim a little.

"What's the hurry? Don't you want me to help do dishes or something?"

Jim turned and shook a rag at Eli. "You have better things to do. Of course, maybe, instead of dinner you'd rather have your romantic book reading."

Eli grinned. "You mean, I don't even get a snack first?"

Jim's eyes twinkled mischievously. "Sure. Some of Anya's cookies, or should I say sugar cubes, are in the pantry."

Eli laughed. "I'll pass."

Eli started to joke about sticking around longer to help with dinner, but when he saw Jim reach for his cane, and knew he would probably be on the receiving end of some motivation from it, he decided it was time to leave. He gathered up his flowers and headed out the door.

He quick-stepped it over to Harris's home. The sun glowed brightly as it descended toward the horizon. Even though it was still quite light, the moon in the eastern sky was plainly visible. The glowing evening sky lit the houses around him in a soft luminescence as he walked. Their Victorian architecture made him feel like he was walking through his hometown in England.

Anya was waiting. She was wearing a different gingham dress. Her hair had a yellow ribbon tied around it at the top, pulling it back from her face and letting it fall loosely down her back. As she smiled at him, Eli thought that she seemed more beautiful every time he saw her.

Eli couldn't wait to get back to eat. He visited briefly with Agnes and Whitman, and then they were on their way. As the door shut behind them, Anya reached down and took his hand before he had a chance to take hers. It felt good to know that she liked to hold his hand, too.

Eli thought how nice it was that people didn't stop and stare now. Almost everyone would look at them, smile, and then go about their business. A couple of old men playing checkers on a porch waved at them, then continued on with their game. Mrs. Klampton stopped to visit about the lemonade for the church bazaar the next day. She frowned at Anya, and Anya shrank back behind him. Mrs. Klampton's view on him marrying someone local had softened slightly, but she and Anya didn't seem to lose any friendliness between them. Mrs. Klampton also still seemed to be nursing a slight grudge against them because of Jim's words to her. Eli was relieved when the conversation had ended and they were on their way again.

When they arrived at Jim's cabin, Eli led Anya into the living room and helped her remove her coat. It was then that he noticed the pictures. Two of

105

them stood on a small desk. One was of a woman and the other was of a small boy. Although the desk was usually cluttered, Eli still knew the pictures had not been there before.

He walked over and picked up the picture of the woman. It was hand drawn. The woman's beautiful brown eyes looked out at him from beneath a wisp of coal black hair that curled across her forehead. She smiled pleasantly.

He then picked up the picture of the boy. He was handsome with a tinge of mischief in his smile. His hair was brown, much like Eli's own.

Eli felt Anya's hand touch his arm, and she looked at him questioningly. She pointed to the picture of the little boy. "Is you?"

Eli shook his head. Suddenly, Jim was standing beside them. He gently took the picture of the woman. "I hadn't looked at these in years, until today. As I was cleaning, I came across them tucked away in a drawer where I put them so long ago when the pain of seeing them tore at my heart. Today I felt it was time to dust them off."

"Is it..." Eli paused.

"Yes," Jim answered. "It's Mary and Jimmy. An artist was traveling through here painting landscapes. He would draw a person's pictures for a small fee. I paid him to make these."

Eli continued to stare at the picture in his hand. Mary and Jimmy suddenly seemed even more real. He had tried to imagine them, and now, here they were, looking out at him from the images on these small canvases.

Anya spoke quietly, as if realizing the importance of these pictures. "Who Mary and Jimmy?"

Eli turned to her to explain. "Mary was Jim's wife, and Jimmy was his son."

The look of surprise shown in Anya's face. "Me at first had thought perhaps Eli Jim's son, but Eli say family far away, so me thought perhaps uncle and had no other family."

Jim smiled. "Eli isn't my real son, though he seems much like one since he came here two years ago."

Eli felt a tightness in his throat. He had often sensed that Jim thought of him as a son, but it was nice to hear him say it. Anya continued with her questions, and Eli was concerned that Jim might get upset, since he had been so stern about sharing it. Even though Jim had opened up about it, Eli hadn't dared delve too deeply. But as Anya continued to query about Mary and Jimmy, Jim didn't seem bothered, though his voice became quiet and sad. "They died many years ago," he explained.

Anya looked as though she would cry. "I sad. Mary and Jimmy beautiful."

Jim nodded. "Yes, they are."

They all stood there quietly for some time. Anya seemed to be grasping the enormity of all of it. There was a quiet reverence to the moment.

It was as if Anya brought a gentleness out in Jim that no one else had been able to. Her quiet compassion seemed to soften him and strengthen him at the same time. Eli found himself marveling at her deep goodness.

Suddenly, Jim seemed to want to change the subject. He put the picture back and turned to the others. "Eli, are you going to stand there all day, or are you going to invite this young lady in for dinner?"

Eli put Jimmy's picture back on the desktop. He took Anya by the hand and led her to the kitchen. He paused at the door for one last look back at the pictures. He couldn't even get his thoughts around the feelings he felt.

Jim invited them to sit down and began dishing up their plates. He started with mashed potatoes, which he mounded into a little bowl, then he filled it with baked beans smothered in tomato sauce. From the oven he took a pan full of chicken sprinkled with garlic, and then he took some sausages that were sizzling on the stove and laid them across the chicken.

As he brought each plate to the table, the smell of the spices made Eli's mouth water until he thought he was going to go crazy. After Jim placed the three plates on the table, he retrieved a pitcher of sarsaparilla that he had cooled in the stream that ran by the cabin. When Eli looked at him quizzically, he just smiled. "Sarsaparilla fresh from the pool hall. I got Bob to donate it."

As soon as Eli had blessed the food, they all dug in. When Eli cut a sausage, Jim pointed a fork at him. "Now, the darker sausages are hot, and the lighter ones are sweet. You'll have to tell me which ones you like best."

Eli took a bite of the dark sausage, and it burned in a pleasant way. His eyes did water slightly, and he reached quickly for the sarsaparilla to wash it down. He took a bite of a lighter sausage, which burst in his mouth with a sweet, honey-like flavor. He tried the chicken, and the garlic teased his tastebuds.

"Jim, this is wonderful. What do you call this?"

Jim grinned. "It is called Chicken Vessuvio."

Eli could see that Anya was thoroughly enjoying her meal. The hot sausages didn't seem to bother her at all. He realized she must be used to it. He had poured her a cold glass of sarsaparilla which, since it had sat a while, didn't have the bubbles that it had down at the pool hall. Eli watched carefully to see what Anya would think of the sarsaparilla. She took a long, deep chug and let out a muffled burp as her eyes widened.

She looked shocked and covered her mouth, but Jim just laughed. "It has that effect on me, too." Anya blushed.

Eli thought he had never tasted anything so exquisite as the chicken, until he got to the beans and potatoes. They mixed in a culinary masterpiece the likes of which Eli had never imagined. He was just finishing up and thinking he would never need to eat again in his entire life, when Jim brought in a beautiful pie topped with lightly browned meringue.

"A pie, Jim?" Eli asked. "I didn't know you could cook like this."

Jim laughed and winked at Eli. "Well, that's because I ain't had no one pretty to cook for in a long time."

Anya blushed again, and Jim laughed as he reached for a big knife to cut the pie. He cut the pie into quarters and put one on each plate. He brought some cold milk in from the stream and poured them each a tall glassful.

Eli bit into his pie, and the sweet, sour mixture melted in his mouth. "Jim, what kind of pie is this?"

Jim grinned. "It's my favorite in all the world. It is called rhubarb, though some people call it pie plant."

"Rhubarb?" Eli thought to himself. Jim grew the plant out behind his cabin. It had long red stocks with huge leaves on top. He had asked Jim about it once. He had heard of it in England, but thought it was just a weed.

Jim explained. "I got a plant from a trader that came through the area. He told me how to make the pie. I made it and couldn't believe how good it was, even before I really got good at making it." Then Jim got real quiet and a warm smile crossed his face. "I made it for Mary the first time I asked her over for dinner."

Both men watched Anya take her first bite of pie. Her eyes grew wide with wonder. She turned to Jim in surprise. "Jim is good cook. Better than Anya."

"If you'll share some of your recipes with me, I'll share some of mine with you," he said.

Anya nodded excitedly, though Eli thought that Jim could probably forgo Anya's cookie recipe. No one had room for the last piece of pie, so they retired to the living room. As they sat down, all eyes drifted back to the pictures.

Anya looked over at Jim. "Tell about Mary and Jimmy?"

Eli held his breath, wondering what Jim would say, but Jim's eyes got soft, and he started to talk about them. He shared lots of stories about the lumber camp and funny things Jimmy did and said. When he got to the part about their deaths, his voice quivered. He didn't tell how he had planned to take his life before Eli came. He just ended with, "I loved them very much."

No one said anything for some time, then Anya said, "I wonder much from I arrive. Now I begin understand more."

Jim told them more stories, some that shocked Eli. Jim had taught himself to play the fiddle in the little village he grew up in in the mountains of Virginia, and had played for barn-raisings and such. He told how his mother had dreams of him going off to a school where he could learn to read and write and study to be a true musician, but he ran away to the sea instead. He found he hated ships so, when the ship landed in Northshore, he stayed and secured a job at the lumber camp when he was only nineteen. He told lots of stories of people in the town, but still seemed to hold back from sharing everything about Jimmy and Mary.

The evening passed quickly. Eli wished it would go on forever. He was enjoying sitting there listening to Jim tell about his life. Eli also enjoyed the feeling of Anya's hand in his. When she had come in on the ship, his life suddenly turned upside down, but now he couldn't imagine life without her or Jim.

When it grew so late that Eli could no longer put off taking Anya home, he helped her with her coat. She smiled at Jim as they left and said, "Goodnight, Jim. Thank you for good dinner and good time." Jim returned her smile. "Goodnight, Anya, and you're welcome."

Eli looked at these two people who now meant more to him than anyone in the world, and thought about how they all three needed each other. He thought about Molly, who didn't have the tenderness that he saw in Anya. Since Molly was boisterous and loud, he wondered if she would have softened Jim like Anya did. Eli had always felt that God had brought him to this place, though he had questioned that assumption when he found out about Molly. But, he was beginning to feel more sure of it all of the time. Maybe, God saw that the woman he needed with him in this place was not Molly, but Anya. Perhaps her gentle goodness was not only what he and Jim needed in their lives, but also what the people of Northshore needed.

He was deep in thought as the two of them walked quietly through the night together. Eli noticed that Anya, too, seemed deep in thought. The sun had long gone down and the moon was already marching its way across the sky. The crickets were singing in full forte, their chorus echoing happily through the cool air. The frogs added a solid bass, and the music of the night was glorious. Anya snuggled up against him, and Eli thought the whole world seemed right. It truly did seem right.

Chapter 19
Fifty Dollars

It was barely after work on Friday, and the town was already abuzz about the church bazaar. It was going to be a big event. Some of the men from the lumber camp were even planning to get spiffed up and come down. Eli hoped George wouldn't be there, and he doubted he would be. George wouldn't recognize a bar of soap if he were introduced to it. Eli had heard some men say that if George washed even once each year, it was only on accident.

It was still a couple of hours before the bazaar, but Eli was heading down to the town hall. He had been doing this every snatch of the day he wasn't with Anya. This time, Jim was accompanying him. They hadn't even taken time to eat a snack after work. Eli had to collect the last of the money he needed tonight. "Besides," he told Jim, "it will just make the food at the bazaar taste that much better."

As they walked through town, Eli could feel the hunger cause his stomach to do flop-flops. He could smell the aroma of the freshly baked pies and cakes wafting out from every door they passed. Women had been busy baking all day, and the smell of rich foods hung over the town like a London fog. Each woman planned to bring one dessert to sell and one food item for the potluck dinner. When they passed one doorway, the scent of roasting turkey drifted out, and Jim voiced Eli's own thoughts when he said, "My stomach is about to climb right out of my throat."

They hurried along as fast as they could, trying to ignore the pleasantries around them. Jim was also carrying some books in one hand as he thumped along with his cane in the other. Eli freed his own arms of their load, setting the books down on the stairs of town hall, and he hurriedly retrieved a table and a few more books from inside. He set up the table and put the books on it. Jim plopped the books he was carrying on the table, then sat down on the stairs.

Many people came by, curiously thumbing through the books, but no one bought anything. As the colors in the sky began to fade, Eli fidgeted more and more. Finally, he turned to Jim. "These books haven't brought in what I had hoped, and the rest just aren't selling."

Jim stood up beside him. "How much do you have?"

Eli pulled the money from his pocket and quickly thumbed through it. He had counted it a thousand times and probably didn't really need to count it again, but it was as if, in counting it, he might find something there that wasn't before. "Just over thirty dollars."

Jim tapped his cane on the ground. "That really should be plenty."

Eli shook his head. "I want ten times what anyone has ever paid for a gratitude dowry for a wife. It's got to be fifty dollars."

"But you're almost out of books and even more out of time. What else can you do?"

Eli spoke resolutely. "I only have two things left."

He turned to look at Jim. Jim must have seen the steel determination in Eli's eyes. Suddenly, he realized what Eli was talking about. He gasped. "Don't tell me you plan to sell them, too! It can't be that important!"

Eli squared his shoulders. "The worth of a human being cannot be measured in gold or silver." He paused a moment and then added, "Nor in a dress or a ring."

"But you've had them in your family for generations," Jim said.

"They are still just possessions," Eli replied.

"I thought your mother gave them to you for your wedding."

Eli nodded. "She did."

"But if you sell them, you won't have them for your wedding."

"I think, in this case, my mother would approve," Eli said.

Jim muttered quietly to himself. "I sure hope so."

Eli put his hand on Jim's shoulder. "I don't have a lot of time. I've got to get the money to the captain. If someone comes, you try to sell these last books, and I'll go get the other items."

Eli hurried off toward home as fast as he could run. When he returned, he carried a beautiful wedding dress and a small box which contained an heirloom ring. Jim turned away as Eli put them on the table. He seemed unable to bear seeing them there. He knew how much they meant to Eli. Eli arranged them lovingly on the table and felt a sadness about them, even as his resolve strengthened.

"Are you sure, Eli?" Jim asked.

Eli nodded. "I've just got to."

It wasn't long before Mabel and Elizabeth came wandering by. Eli thought to himself that there might have been a better pair of people to sell to, but he also knew that Mabel and Elizabeth had an eye for pretty things. They were deep in conversation. Mabel was mad about something. They could hear her long before she approached their small table. "...going fishing, he says. You are not going fishing, I tell him."

"I would say not," Elizabeth answered. "Why, I..."

Eli interrupted them, afraid they would pass by and not see what he was selling. "Ladies, could I interest you in a beautiful dress or a ring?"

Mabel eyed Eli suspiciously. "Why, Eli, I thought you were saving those for your wedding."

Eli nodded. "Yes, but I have something more important I need the money for."

Mabel and Elizabeth turned to each other, and their eyes met in a suspicious glance.

Elizabeth raised her eyebrows. "And just what would that be?"

"I'd rather not say. It's going to be a surprise."

Mabel turned to Elizabeth. "I bet it is!"

Elizabeth cleared her throat. "How much do you want for them?"

Eli looked at the two items, then over at Jim, and back at the items again. He looked up at the ladies. "Ten dollars apiece."

Jim frowned at this. Eli had told him about them and he knew they were worth far more than that, but Eli was just trying to reach his goal of fifty dollars.

Mabel slid her purse behind herself. "Ten dollars. It's not like a person carries that much around."

Elizabeth fingered the silky fabric of the wedding dress. "They are beautiful."

Eli nodded. "My mother sent them with me. They are family heirlooms."

Mabel picked up the ring from its box and turned it over in her hand. "I can't believe you would part with them."

"I don't want to, but I must."

Mabel's voice became very business like. "Well, if you must. I'll give you five dollars for the ring."

Elizabeth patted the dress. "And I'll give you five for the wedding dress."

Eli shook his head. "I'm sorry ladies. It's got to be ten dollars. I can't take a penny less."

Mabel put her hand on her hip. "I see. And how much are you trying to raise?"

Eli looked from one lady to the other. "Fifty dollars total."

Elizabeth smiled slyly. "I suppose we could help you out a bit. I'll give you fifteen dollars for both of them."

Mabel turned to look at Elizabeth as if she was considering murder. "Now wait a minute! I was the first to see the ring." She turned back to Eli. "I'll go ahead and give you twenty dollars for both of them."

Elizabeth pushed Mabel aside. "I'll give you twenty four."

Mabel shoved her back and grabbed at the dress for herself. "Some friend you are. I'll give you..."

Jim seemed afraid that there was going to be a fight and either the dress or the ring would be ruined. He stepped up and pointed his cane menacingly at the two ladies. "Now, hold on. What if each of you paid Eli twelve dollars for the first item you asked about? That way he could have the money he needs and have enough to take Anya some place special."

The ladies paused and Mabel looked over at Elizabeth then took a deep breath. "Make it eleven, and it's a deal." .

Eli grinned. "All right."

The ladies dug through their purses and handed him the money. The ladies each retrieved their own purchase and, as they were leaving, Eli busily started counting the money.

"... fifty-one, fifty-two, fifty-two-twenty-five. Jim! Jim! I've got it!"

Jim smiled weakly. "And a little extra. I should have let them keep bidding. You might have really made a killing."

"It doesn't matter," Eli said. "I've got the money. Here's the plan. We're going fishing tomorrow, so after we are done I'll pay the captain. Then I'll take her out to dinner. I'll tell her what I've done and ask her to marry me. I can't wait to see the look on her face."

Jim nodded. "Yes, that will be something to see."

Suddenly, Eli panicked. "Jim, here comes Anya now."

They hurriedly gathered everything up and carried it into the town hall. Jim started setting books into the little bookcase while Eli acted like he was calmly setting up for the bazaar. As Anya stepped into town hall she called out. "Hello?"

Eli went to greet her. "Hello, Anya."

"Hello, Eli." She held out a plate of cookies and smiled at him. "I brought cookies to sell."

Eli looked at the plate of cookies and, remembering the last ones, smiled weakly back. "Uh, how nice."

Jim, finished stuffing the books in the bookcase and turned around. "Well, I suppose I better be heading home and get the things we made for the bazaar."

"Oh, Jim," Eli said, holding out the plate of cookies, "how about I buy you a cookie to start out the bazaar?" Eli knew Jim was very hungry.

Jim reached for one, "Sure, that would be nice. There's nothing like a ..." He stopped. He turned and looked at Anya, obviously remembering the last cookies that were so full of sugar they wrapped around his teeth like hardened molasses. "Wait a minute. Who cooked them?"

Anya smiled shyly as Eli, grinning, motioned toward Anya. "Who do you think?

Jim looked back and forth between the two of them. He frowned at Eli. "Oh, no. I couldn't ask you to spend your hard earned money on something for me."

Eli pushed the plate into Jim's chest. "I insist."

Jim reluctantly took one and scowled at Eli. "You got yours comin', you know."

Then he thumped his way home.

Anya watched Jim go out the door. "Jim funny man."

Eli nodded. "Yes, he is."

Eli dropped a penny into the collection jar. He began preparations for the bazaar. There was a lot to do. He had to build a fire, though he wasn't sure it would do much good with lots of people going in and out. Still, if a person wanted to come up and warm themselves, they could. There were tables to set up, chairs to unfold, and the kitchen to get ready.

Anya had volunteered to help, and Eli had gladly accepted. Eli worked setting up the tables and smiled as he watched her busily setting up chairs around the room. He thoroughly enjoyed her company, and she was always willing to help. He knew she would be a good wife.

The thought of having her as his wife made the excitement about tomorrow continue to mount in his heart, and it was all he could do to keep from telling her now.

Chapter 20
The Bazaar

The bazaar was organized to raise the remainder of the money for the new bell that would serve as both a church and school bell. It had already been ordered with a down payment. Since everyone considered Eli the town preacher, he obviously couldn't miss the bazaar. In fact, he had planned this for months. He had thought that there could be no better way for everyone to meet his wife than to have a church social, and why not get the bell paid off at the same time?

He had planned it all out. He would marry Molly early in the week, and then everyone could come to the bazaar and meet her. He looked at Anya. Well, maybe they could still meet his future wife. He thought perhaps he was assuming a lot, but she seemed to want to stay with him. Why else would she want to help him set up?

The thought briefly crossed his mind that she still might want to leave, perhaps head on to California. But the thought yanked so hard at his heart that he put it quickly out of his mind. Maybe he should ask her to marry him now, so he could tell everyone she was his fiancée. No, he wanted it to be a special moment, their moment - just he and Anya. He didn't want to ask her hurriedly.

By the time the tables and chairs were set up, the first people were starting to arrive. Agnes was among them, carrying a three-layered, chocolate cake for the auction. Whitman followed close behind with a large pan of fried chicken for the dinner. The smell of the chicken made the saliva flow in Eli's mouth, and he had to grit his teeth to stop himself from snitching a piece.

Mr. Klampton arrived with some men bringing barrels of lemonade. As Mrs. Klampton came in carrying a large pot roast, Eli made a mental note to help Anya as she got her food for dinner. He had already learned from Agnes about Anya's aversion to beef, and he didn't want her to get some by mistake, ruining the evening for her

Soon the place was full and food filled the tables. The smell of hams, chicken, roast, creamed potatoes, and baked beans filled the air. As Eli walked the length of the table, he could see corn bread with a plate of butter and a bowl of honey nearby. There was cooked corn, cooked carrots, a large turkey, and mounds and mounds of mashed potatoes with creamy butter. The food went on and on. At the end of the table were the pitchers of cold lemonade. The dinner was only a quarter per person, but the desserts were purchased by the item or auctioned off.

The men at the lumber camp spilled into the hall. Eli was relieved to see that George was not among them. Some of the men, like George, wouldn't be caught dead at a church gathering of any kind, even a social.

A lot of sailors were there, including Victor. A group of men stood behind him, and Eli assumed they were his crew.

The hall filled so full that Eli looked with concern at the tables of food. Even with the giant mounds, he wasn't sure there would be enough. He definitely knew there weren't enough plates and utensils, and realized everyone would have to eat in shifts. He went in to get the stacks of plates and utensils from the kitchen, and Anya was there immediately to help him. As they started carrying out what was needed, Agnes signaled to other women, and soon, there was a small army going in and out of the kitchen. It wasn't long before every plate, every bowl, every cup, every saucer, and basically anything a person could use for eating was at the head of the table where the lines were to be formed.

When the hour finally arrived, Eli was working his way to the end of the hall to start the social and offer a blessing on the food, when someone yelled, "Hurry up, already, Preacher, before we all die of hunger!"

Everyone laughed. Eli smiled and began. "We'd like to welcome everyone to the church bazaar. The meal is only a quarter, with two dollars maximum per family. We will have the auction of baked goods and homemade items afterward, along with the dance. It all goes to a good cause - our new church and school bell, so we hope everyone will be generous. Please deposit your money in the jar and form lines down both sides of the tables. We'll wash dishes as quickly as we can to give everyone a chance to eat. I will now offer a prayer."

After Eli finished the prayer, there was some good natured jostling for position in line, and a din of happy chatter filled the room. Eli realized that since he had been in North Shore, there had never been a town social, though this hall was obviously built for that purpose. The men went to the pool hall and the women had their teas. He wondered why a building built for that purpose was not utilized. Yet, he knew it must have been used before, because everything in the kitchen showed lots of wear. But why were there no socials anymore?

As Eli's mind came back to the present, he looked at Anya. She had stayed right by his side all night. Although a few people stared at her, she was beginning to fit in. Everyone seemed to be accepting her, even Janice Klampton, though grudgingly. He remembered how hard it was for him to fit in - him with his ideas and expectations that were so different from others here.

He was thinking that, perhaps, this truly was home, and he was feeling quite contented, when the dirty dishes started piling up, waking him from his happy thoughts. Earlier, he had built a fire in the kitchen's cookstove and put on some water to boil. He had asked for volunteers for many jobs, but he had put himself on dish duty, feeling it was the worst assignment. He didn't want anyone to think he wouldn't do what he asked of others.

He told Anya where he was going, and headed to the kitchen with a load of plates. He had no sooner rolled up his sleeves, grabbing the pan of hot water to pour into the sink, than Anya was there, rolling up her sleeves, as well. "I help."

Eli nodded. He poured some hot water into both sinks, and then he poured some cooler water from a big bucket on the counter. He put soap in one sink.

Although things were different for Anya, she had learned from Agnes how people here worked in a kitchen, and she jumped right in. Eli washed and put them into the rinse water. Anya would pull them out and dry them. They would no sooner have a stack of plates, utensils, and cups ready than they were being whisked out, and a new load of dirty ones were being brought in.

Agnes came in once and smiled, seeing them working side by side. She tied an apron around Anya and found a ribbon with which she tied Anya's hair back. She patted Eli on the shoulder and headed back out into the hall.

Once, Eli saw little beads of sweat forming on Anya's forehead and an intent look on her face as she efficiently wiped each plate. He began to feel that, perhaps, Jim and Whitman were right. Maybe God did answer his prayers differently than he had planned. Sure, Molly was the life of the party, but he couldn't imagine her here in the kitchen doing dishes.

He was different than the man that had left England two years ago. That was a young man who enjoyed parties and social life. Now, he was a man people looked to for other things - more important things. The man that he had become would not have done well with Molly. But as he looked at Anya, her beauty showing through the sweat rolling down her face, he knew he couldn't do better than her.

As the dishes started to slow, Eli figured everyone was finishing their meal. Thinking he heard the band warming up, he grabbed Anya by the hand and led her back out into the hall. Sure enough, the band was getting ready. They had pulled two tables together against the end wall for a stage, and they stood on these preparing their instruments. Whitman had his harmonica, Fred Jackson was on a washboard, Andrew Jaimison was playing the saw and, to Eli's utter astonishment, Jim was warming up on a fiddle.

"Jim, you're going to play the fiddle?" Eli asked.

Jim grinned. "I'm full of surprises. I told you my mother wanted me to be a musician. When Whitman volunteered to get a band together, he asked me. At first I told him no. I hadn't played since Mary died, and I told him I didn't have the heart. But this week I changed my mind, and I've practiced every day, almost all day, while you've been at work."

Eli was flabbergasted. He had never seen Jim smiling and excited like this, and he wasn't the only one surprised. Some of the men from the camp stood around, mouths gaping wide open, like a specter had floated into the room. But when Jim pulled a long draw across the strings, sounding like the long whistle of a ship, it was real, all right, and it was the signal for the others to join in. The music vibrated around the hall with a pulsating rhythm.

The dance floor seemed to come alive as people poured onto it. As Eli stood, wide-eyed, Agnes stepped up beside him. "Bet you didn't know this town could dance?" Eli shook his head. "We used to have dances almost every Friday night," Agnes continued, "but when Mary died, Jim quit, and without him there really was no band. There's hardly been a social in this town since that day." As Eli continued to watch in shock, and was taking in what Agnes was saying, she continued. "If you think he is good now, you should have seen him then. Years ago Jim was the life of the party and a big part of the life of this town. In some ways, when Mary died, Jim's spirit died with her and, with it, went the vibrancy of North Shore." Eli choked back his feelings as Agnes finished. "Something in you and Anya has brought the life back to him."

Eli had seen how Jim responded to Anya's compassion and knew that Jim was seeing Eli and Anya as a son and a daughter. He again realized that Molly, with her high spirits, would not have been able to do that. But what if Anya decided not to stay? Could God bring her here, only to take her away again? The thought seemed so ridiculous he excused it from his mind.

As Eli watched the skirts swirling and the boots tapping, a warm, happy feeling spread over him. He looked up at Jim, grinning, playing the fiddle, and Eli felt all was as it should be.

Then, he was aware again of Anya, as she touched his arm, and the rumble coming from his stomach reminded him that he hadn't eaten, and neither had she. He led her to the table of food. As he reached up to drop fifty cents into the jar for them he felt a hand on his shoulder. There stood Victor and the foreman from the lumber camp, each holding a quarter. "Our treat," the foreman said, and they each dropped a quarter into the jar.

Eli nodded a thank you, and Anya smiled at the two men. There was plenty left, although pickings were slim on some items. He was disappointed to find that Agnes's chicken was gone, but there was still plenty of ham and turkey. They filled their plates to heaping and sat in some chairs along the wall. The food was good, and it didn't take them long to put it away.

Eli got them each a glass of the lemonade from the pitchers dipped from the barrels furnished by Klampton's General store. It had ice in it and real lemon slices. Eli saw Anya's eyes widened as she took a sip, and then she downed it quickly. She realized he was watching her, and she blushed. He just smiled and got her a refill.

Seconds were free, and they returned and filled their plates again. They worked their way though the second helping much more slowly, and Eli knew he better quit, or he'd be sick.

He took Anya by the hand and asked her to dance. She hesitated a moment and, by the look in her eye, he knew she was unsure. "Have you ever danced before?" She shook her head. "Would you like to learn?" She nodded uncertainly, and he took her gently by the hand and lead her to a secluded corner of the dance floor near the band.

He put his arm around her and positioned her hands on his shoulder and arm. He attempted to show her a few simple waltz steps, but his own clumsiness hindered and frustrated him. He had often thought himself a good dancer, but he realized he was rather awkward. It had been Molly who was graceful, and she had made him look good. He hadn't danced for two years, and he felt more than a little inept. He looked at Anya and, though he didn't wish Molly in her place, he wished he could bring back some of that magic he had shared with her on the dance floors of England.

The music stopped, and people were staring in their direction. Jim's eyes met his, and then Jim nodded to the others in the band, and they set down their instruments. Each of the three men stepped down and held their hands out to their wives. Jim put the fiddle to his chin and started to play a waltz step that Eli remembered from his days with Molly. It was then that Eli realized he had been trying to teach a waltz step to music that was not a waltz. Everyone joined in on the dance floor, and Anya's eyes were wide with wonder watching the gracefulness of men and women waltzing together.

Whitman and Agnes glided over beside them, and Anya watched Agnes. Awkwardly, but together, Eli and Anya moved, following Agnes and Whitman's lead.

Jim soloed one more waltz and, before it ended, Eli and Anya were gliding nicely together. When the music stopped, it was time for the auction.

Eli knew Whitman was going to be the auctioneer, but, as he was about to step forward, Agnes whispered something to him and pointed at Jim. Whitman nodded and quietly talked to Jim. Jim stood, paused for a moment and then nodded. Whitman went back over by his wife.

Jim stepped up to the front of the makeshift stage. "I have been asked to be the auctioneer, so you all gather round and open your wallets."

There was an audible gasp. Eli had to choke back the surprise in his own throat. Agnes whispered, "Jim used to always be the auctioneer. Nobody could get more out of an auction than he could."

Eli stood frozen to the spot, forgetting that it was his job to get the things for Jim to auction off. With a nudge from Agnes, he came to his senses and picked up her three layered chocolate cake.

Jim raised his hand. "We have a chocolate cake here baked by Agnes Harris. We all know how well she can cook, so I am going to start the bidding at twenty-five cents myself. Anyone give me fifty cents?" A man raised his hand in the back. Jim continued on. "I got fifty who will a give me seventy-five, seventy-five, got a seventy-five," Jim said pointing to another raised hand. "Who will give me a dollar?" Jim continued. Jim pointed at Whitman. "Whitman, isn't this your wife's cake?" Whitman nodded. "Then why aren't you bidding? You didn't put something in it, did you?"

Everyone laughed, and Whitman shook his head. "No, but why should I bid when I can get her to make one for me at home?"

Everyone laughed again, but, with a nudge in the ribs from Agnes, Whitman put up a dollar bid. The cake finally went to Fred Jackson for a dollar and a quarter. "Would you like to buy the other two layers of the cake with the first one you just bought?" Jim teased, as Fred came up to pay for the cake. The hall again echoed with laughter. Eli was so shocked at what he was seeing in Jim that he again forgot to retrieve the next item for bid.

As the pile of baked goods was whittling down, Eli found Anya's plate of cookies hidden among the desserts. He knew he had distinctly put them on the table to be sold by the cookie, but, here they were, with a couple missing. Actually, there were a couple of halves missing. Eli figured somebody must have bought them, got a taste, and donated them to the baked food sale.

He didn't know quite what to do. He couldn't put them back on the other table now, and he couldn't let Anya think he didn't want to bid on them. But if he bid too much, he wouldn't have enough to take her to dinner tomorrow. He paused a little too long and finally Jim said, "Eli, what's next?"

Eli held up the plate. "Anya's cookies."

He looked at Jim, hoping he would keep the price down. Jim seemed to understand and nodded as he started the bidding. "We have here a plate of cookies baked by Anya. Now, Anya is learning how to cook here with things being different than she is used to, but isn't it nice she would help out." Anya smiled shyly, as everyone clapped. "Do I hear a bid of twenty-five cents for this plate of cookies?"

Eli's hand immediately shot up, everyone laughed, and Anya smiled.

"Do I have fifty-cents? Who will give me fifty-cents?" Jim continued.

From the back, a hand went up. It was John Jaimison. Jim smiled. "You, know, maybe we ought to let the bidders try a small bite. What do you say John?"

John nodded, and worked his way to the front. Jim broke off a small bite and gave it to him. John thoughtfully started to chew. His eyes widened and told the whole story. He tried about three times to swallow, before he got it down. He turned to Eli. "You, know, the preacher boy ain't got a lot of money, and I'd hate to not have him get the cookies. I'm retracting my bid."

Jim smiled and nodded. "Anybody else want to bid?" Everyone had seen the look on John's face, and nobody moved. "Well, then," Jim continued. "They go to Eli for twenty-five cents."

Eli handed over his quarter for Jim to put in the jar and everyone started to tease him. John Jaimison slapped him on the back. "Good luck with those. You'll need it."

The auction continued on. There were homemade blankets and some carved items. Even Jim had carved a walking stick adorned with faces, much like he had on his own cane. Eli really wanted it. He started out the bidding, but it soon was out of his price range, considering he wanted to use his money to take Anya to dinner the next day.

When the auction ended, the band picked up again for the second half of the dance. Eli danced with Anya some more. She was getting better but still seemed nervous. She seemed to like having Eli's arms around her, but dancing, with men and women touching in public, seemed foreign to her. They took a break from dancing, and Eli slipped over and got her another glass of lemonade. He loved to see her sip it. The rapture on her face pleased him.

As the evening was winding down and people were leaving, Eli decided he better get a jump on finishing the dishes. Anya again joined him in the kitchen. Some ladies had already gone to work on them, and there wasn't a lot left to do.

They finished in the kitchen, then went out to put the tables and chairs away. Jim, Agnes, Whitman, and a few others helped. Eli and Anya swept. Everyone was visiting cheerfully, except for Anya, who was still rather quiet.

They counted the money and found it was more than they had expected and much more than enough to cover the remainder of the bill for the new bell. Eli gave it to Whitman to make the payment. Agnes cued the stragglers, and everyone left Eli and Anya to lock up.

After he had locked the door, he looked at Anya. It was just past midnight, and the moon was blue and beautiful. Its light shimmered off of her hair. She snuggled up close as he put his arm around her. She leaned against him as they walked.

Neither one spoke. Eli thought about the night. In many ways, he felt more comfortable with Anya than he had with Molly. It all seemed so right. In his heart, he said, "Thank you, Lord, for answering my prayers in the way you saw best."

On the horizon the aurora borealis again shimmered and danced. The purples, blues, and reds glowed and trembled across the evening sky, but Eli didn't notice them. Nor did he see the gathering storm clouds in the west.

Chapter 21
Is It Love?

As Anya prepared to go fishing with Eli Saturday morning, she had a lot on her mind. She had enjoyed that thing they called a bazaar. The food was wonderful and that lemonade was so good.

Her thoughts turned to Eli. He had worked in the kitchen washing dishes, sweeping floors, helping with the food. It was true that men were different here from the men in her village, but Eli was different even from them. He was the only man that worked in the kitchen. He did not seem to distinguish something as a "woman's job". If it was work he could help with, he was there helping.

He hadn't even asked her to help, let alone demanded. But when she had offered, he seemed glad to have her with him. It had felt good to work beside him - almost like they were part of each other.

Everyone in town seemed to like and respect Eli. She could see that in the way they treated him. She had wondered why people called him "the preacher", and she finally asked Agnes, who told her that it was because he promoted the interest in having a church in town. She had come to understand that Eli had a strong belief in God, yet he was different from the religious leaders she was used to. In her village, religious leaders were paid for their preaching and their work within the religion. Eli worked hard all day, and then he did these other things, too. Agnes told her that Eli didn't get any money for the religious work, nor did he get anything for teaching people to read and write. He did it because he felt it was right.

Last night, as she was wiping dishes, she would glance over at him. The muscles from hard work rippled in his arms, and he had dish soap to his elbows. It almost made her laugh. No man at home would have been found like that, and few even here. Eli didn't worry much about what others thought, but just considered what was the right thing to do. It made her feelings for him even stronger.

She had been glad when he took her to get some food. She was hungry, and she knew he must be hungry, too. She remembered Eli's shock when Jim played in the band. She could sense something in Jim was different than when she first met him. She had sensed a sadness in his eyes that she couldn't explain, but it seemed to be lifting from him.

She remembered the dinner at Jim's cabin. She couldn't describe the feelings she felt as Jim had described his love for Mary and Jimmy. It was much like what she was beginning to feel for Eli. She had felt a longing for a father like Jim, because she could sense the goodness of his heart. The meal he had cooked was like nothing she had ever tasted before. The spices in the hot sausages reminded her of home, but women seldom ever ate any good meat - only tough, chewy pieces. The chicken had just melted in her mouth. She laughed to herself, as she thought about drinking sarsaparilla. She hadn't meant to burp, but it came up so suddenly. At home, that would have brought rebuke, but Jim and Eli just laughed.

It seemed that Eli and Jim both enjoyed having her experience things that were new to her. She thought of the lemonade at the bazaar. It had tasted so good that she had quickly gulped it down, and then she was embarrassed. But Eli just smiled at her and got her another glass full. She tried to watch him and sip the second glass like he did.

Then there was the dancing. It seemed to her the strangest of all. In her village, the men danced, sometimes drunkenly, in the same room. Once in a while they would bring in a woman to dance for them, most disrespectfully. But never did a man dance with a woman.

At first she had felt reluctant to appear in public with a man that way, even if it was Eli. She wondered if it could be appropriate. But everyone else was doing it, and after Agnes and Whitman started gliding in step with each other, it was beautiful to see, and looked as if it was as it should be. She watched Agnes and tried to imitate her. The oneness she felt with Eli, as they moved together, was a wonderful feeling. His arms around her as they stepped in time to the music made her heart grab the breath from her throat.

Eli had bought her cookies at the auction. She looked at the other food being sold and knew hers didn't look as good. At first, she was embarrassed when her small plate was brought out, but when Eli quickly bid and then bought them, it made her happy - happy that he would buy them even though there were more beautiful foods.

She thought of their walks home together - his arm around her, and her leaning her head against his strong shoulders. She felt so secure and at peace with everything around her. Surely, he would want to marry her. He said he didn't own her, but she found herself wanting to be his more than anything she had ever wanted in her entire life.

But, the ship left tomorrow, and still, he had not said he would marry her nor had he shown any indication that he would pay the gratitude dowry. Was there something that made him reluctant about it? Was he still wishing she was more than she was? She trembled at the thought. The more she thought about how wonderful Eli was, the more she was sure he could never really be satisfied with her. She also knew that, if he did send her away, it would tear her heart to pieces, for she was more sure all of the time that the feelings she had for him was this love he kept talking about.

Yes, she knew she was in love with him.

Chapter 22
Fishing

"So, you have never been fishing before?" Eli asked in surprise, as he prepared to bait the hook.

"No. Only men fish," Anya replied.

"Fishing is lots of fun. Of course, half of the fun is just relaxing by the edge of the water," Eli explained.

Anya smiled eagerly. "I like eat fish."

"Me, too."

The morning was clear and cool and the sun was already well on its journey overhead. The sky was cloudless except for some thistle down clouds here and there and some darker ones along the horizon. It was a perfect day to be out fishing.

Eli opened the bait box and pulled out a big worm. "First we need to bait the hook."

Anya's cheeks completely lost all color and she looked like she was about to lose her breakfast. "Fish eat that?"

"Yes."

Anya swallowed hard. "And we eat fish?"

"Yes."

"I not sure I like eat fish anymore," Anya gagged covering her mouth.

It was all Eli could do to refrain from grinning. He thoughtfully returned the worm to its coffee can and opened another container. "How about we use some corn? We'll catch the fish that like corn."

"I think better fish like corn," Anya agreed enthusiastically.

Eli baited the hook with corn and commenced the lesson. "All right, now. You pull out some line," Eli demonstrated. "Then, you bring the pole back behind you and let go of the line as you cast it forward." He brought the line forward and the string buzzed out of the reel. A perfect cast. He turned to look at Anya, and noticed she was staring at him in a way that only Molly had done before. As their eyes met, she lowered them bashfully. "I'll set it up and you try," he said.

He reeled in the line and handed her the pole. She took it and cautiously pulled out a little line, as she had seen him do. "Like this?" she asked.

"Yes. Now, bring the pole back and, as you toss it forward, you let go of the line," Eli explained.

Anya brought the pole back hard and fast, but, instead of bringing it over her shoulder, she swung it hard right, whacking Eli swiftly across the head. Throwing it forward, she let go of the pole, sending it sailing into the water.

The blow caught Eli by surprise, striking him hard enough to knock him to his backside. Anya gasped, and looked as though she were going to cry. "I sorry!"

Eli shook his head to clear the dizziness and stood up. "It's all right."

Anya looked scared. "I no mean hurt Eli."

"I know. I'll be fine. I'll get the pole." Eli took off his shoes and socks, pulling his pant legs up so he could wade into the water. As his foot touched the icy water, he gasped for air. He continued to breathe hard as he waded out to the pole.

He came back, shivering, with it in hand. "I'll tell you what. Why don't I cast, and I'll let you fish?"

"That good idea," Anya agreed with relief.

Eli put his shoes and socks back on, and then he worked to clear the line that had knotted around the pole. Anya watched patiently. He soon had the line cleared but he had to rebait the hook, since the force of the blow had dislodged the corn.

After it was all ready, he threw a beautiful cast out into the water and handed the pole to her. "Here you go."

She held it gingerly. "Now what I do?"

"You wait for a bite, and when you feel it jiggle like this," Eli said, reaching out and jostling the pole, "then you give it a big jerk to set the hook."

Anya's grip stiffened slightly. "Hold like this?"

Eli nodded. "Yes. Steady." He got behind her so he could see any dip in the pole and avoid a whack like the one he took when he was standing beside her. Suddenly the pole dipped. "There's a wiggle, jerk it!" Eli hollered.

Startled, Anya jerked the pole back hard over her shoulder, whacking Eli across the top of the head and tossing a fish into the bushes. Eli was knocked flat to the ground. Anya quickly threw the pole down and ran to him. "I sorry. Me think fishing not good for person's health."

Eli rubbed the lump that was forming on his head. "Not mine, anyway." Then he grinned, "It was probably worse for the fish, though. I think you probably jerked its lips right off."

Anya helped Eli to his feet. He followed the line and found a good-sized fish still flipping on the hook. Anya was both excited and repulsed by the fish at the same time. As it wriggled, Eli could see by the look on her face that she might get sick. He made a mental note to clean the fish at home, where she wouldn't see.

"I'll tell you what. Let me help you through all of it," Eli suggested.

"All right," Anya said.

Eli readied the pole and then guided Anya in front of him. He put his arms around her and helped her work out some line. With his hand on hers, he helped her cast. It was a good cast, though not as good as he could have done alone, but still sufficiently far. He stayed there, with his arm around her, holding the pole.

"Now," he said, "when we feel that little nibble, we jerk." The pole dipped slightly and they managed a unified jerk. He shook his head. "Oh, shoot. We missed."

Anya leaned her head back against Eli. "I like fishing."

Eli felt her soft black hair smooth against his face. "Me too," he said. Before long the pole dipped sharply. Together they jerked the pole. "There, we got one," Eli said. He loosed his grip a little on her hand, allowing her to reel it in with only a small amount of coaching. "Careful. Careful."

They fished that way all morning and into the afternoon, stopping only briefly for something to eat. At lunch time they took the trail backwards that they had taken that night from the lumber camp, stopping near an outcropping of rock on a grassy knoll in a clearing high above the ocean. It seemed they could see half way around the world from there. The day was calm and peaceful, except for the seagulls begging down by the fishing boats, and the sound of the waves crashing against the shore.

The sun sparkled over the water, making it look like a giant blue diamond mine with facets of shimmering prisms. The salty air flowing up from the bay smelled fresh and clean.

Jim had packed them some egg salad sandwiches and cookies, which he had made with the hope that Anya would see that extra sugar didn't necessarily improve the taste. They ate with great gusto. Eli enjoyed watching Anya eat.

He thought about his sisters. When they went to a party, they ate prim and proper amounts, pretending to be delicate. But, when they were home, they were ravenous, and he had to fight them for his fair share. Anya didn't make any pretense. She ate heartily. He wondered if it was partially because of having gone hungry, but he felt it was more likely because she never gave any pretense as to what she was, and was always just herself. He liked that in her.

They returned to fishing and fished until they had a good catch and the sun was getting high enough that the fish had quit biting. They were also getting low on corn, and Eli knew he couldn't bait the hooks with worms.

As they walked back to Harris's house, he issued her an invitation to dine out, informing her there was something he wanted to tell her. His excitement was building, until he thought he would explode, but he wanted to wait until they were having their candlelight dinner together.

He had no sooner dropped her off, than he headed down to the dock to pay the captain. His heart was light and happy. He was so excited that he didn't notice Mabel and Elizabeth following him, nor had he noticed that they had kept an eye on him and Anya all day, even while they were fishing. Nor did he notice them turn and head for Harris's house after they saw him pay the captain. His heart was so full of happiness that his only thoughts were for Anya. He didn't even see the storm that was now coming out of the clear sky, rolling quickly and darkly in their direction, thundering with an ominous fury that was about to be unleashed.

Chapter 23
Trouble

As Anya walked in, she was humming happily. She couldn't believe Eli could be such a wonderful person. Even when she had accidentally hurt him, he didn't yell or get angry. At home such an action would have brought immediate and horrible consequences.

Agnes looked up from her knitting and smiled. "Did you have fun?"

Anya grinned. "Yes. We went fishing."

"Did you catch anything?"

"Yes. Eli catch fish and let me pull it in."

Agnes was shocked. "Didn't you have your own pole?"

Anya looked at her with surprise. "Own pole?'

Agnes nodded. "Yes. When Whitman and I go fishing, we each take our own pole."

Anya frowned, remembering leaning back against Eli with his arms so warmly around her. "That no sound fun. Eli help me fish much more fun."

"You've never fished before?"

"No, but is so exciting." She pretended to cast and then pull in a fish, as if in a daydream. Then, coming back to reality, she turned to Agnes. "Must change now."

"You going somewhere?"

"Yes. Eli and I go place make out."

Agnes was out of her chair in an instant. "You're going to do what?" She had heard a few young teenagers use that phrase, but she never expected it from Eli.

Agnes's sudden shock surprised Anya. She was much quieter as she explained. "Eli say we eat out and tell me something important."

The relief on Agnes's face was evident. "Oh! You are going to eat out. Where is he taking you?"

Anya shook her head. "I not know. Someplace make out. I not taste out before."

Agnes smiled at Anya's innocence. "No, Anya. To eat out means to eat out of your home."

"Out mean like eat outside? I need dress warm?" Anya queried.

Agnes put her arm around her. "No. It means you will eat at a restaurant."

Anya tried to repeat the word. "Rest ront?"

"Yes. A restaurant is a place that cooks so you don't have to. You sit there and eat by candlelight. It is so romantic," Agnes sighed.

Anya's eyes lit up. She had heard Agnes, Mabel, and Elizabeth talk about romantic things and knew this was good, though she wasn't quite sure what it meant. "Oh. How I dress?"

Agnes gave her a little squeeze. "In your most beautiful dress."

Anya slipped off to her room excitedly. "I hurry."

Agnes had just settled back into her chair and pulled her knitting onto her lap, when there was a loud, anxious knock at the door. She got up to answer it and was surprised to find Mabel and Elizabeth standing there - quite unusual for a Saturday afternoon. She stepped back from the door and motioned to them. "Mabel, Elizabeth. Come in. Come in. It's good to see you."

Mabel had a surly look on her face. "You may not think so, after what we have to tell you."

Agnes's eyebrows furrowed as she looked from one to the other. "What is it?"

Elizabeth took a deep breath, as if trying to dramatize the moment, even though it was obvious she could hardly wait to tell the news. "You had better sit down."

Agnes sat and motioned to some chairs. "You go ahead and have a seat, too."

The two ladies pulled some chairs up close, like vultures moving in as the suspense built. Agnes again looked from one lady to the other. "What could be so important?"

Mabel swallowed hard, pretending that what she had to say was hard for her. "We have just realized why Eli has been selling all of his things."

"And why is that?"

Mabel took a deep breath. "He is planning to send Anya home."

Agnes shook her head. "You must be mistaken. Eli cares greatly for Anya."

Elizabeth folded her arms. "We just know what we've seen and heard."

Mabel jumped in. "We were pretty sure of this yesterday, but we wanted to be really sure, so we watched him today."

Elizabeth nodded. "It actually started last night."

"Yes," Mabel said, "he was trying to sell the wedding ring he has been saving."

Agnes gasped. "The wedding ring?"

Elizabeth nodded. "You know, the one his mother gave him for his future wife."

"Not only that," Mabel said, "but he sold the wedding dress, too. Everyone in town knows he was saving them for his wedding day."

"Who did he sell them to?" Agnes asked.

"Well, um, I bought the ring," Mabel said.

Elizabeth's face flushed red. "And I bought the wedding dress."

Agnes's voice sounded disgusted. "What do you want with a wedding dress?"

Elizabeth sounded annoyed. "I do have daughters, you know. And it is very beautiful."

Agnes shook her head. "Still, selling those things does not mean he plans to send her home."

Mabel looked over at Elizabeth and nodded. "That's what we said. That's why we watched him all day."

Agnes's voice got stern. "But he was with Anya all day."

Elizabeth shook her finger. "Uh, uh, uh. He was with Anya most of the day! After he brought her here, we followed him."

Agnes looked at her questioningly. "And?"

"And he went down to the ship and bought a ticket," Mabel said.

Suddenly, from behind them, Anya gasped. They turned to see her, hand over her mouth, looking as if she was going to cry. It was obvious she had heard it all. She was holding a dress in front of her like she was going to ask if it was the one she should wear.

Her voice quivered. "Eli bought ticket?"

Elizabeth nodded. "I'm afraid so."

Agnes turned to the ladies and scowled. "Are you sure it was a ticket?"

Elizabeth jumped in. "He said he had to raise fifty dollars."

Mabel shook her finger to emphasize the point. "And we saw him give the captain a large sum of money and an envelope, and then the captain handed him a piece of paper. What else could it be?"

Agnes took a deep breath, as she looked at Anya. "It could be a..." She paused and shook her head. "I don't know."

Elizabeth's expression hardened. "Face the facts. That's all it could be."

Agnes looked bewildered. "But this isn't like Eli."

Mabel's frown deepened. "He's a man, isn't he? And all men are alike. You just can't trust them."

Elizabeth let out a light sigh. "I bet he had no intention of ever marrying her."

Anya burst into tears and ran from the room.

Agnes spoke quietly. "I wish you hadn't said that in front of Anya."

Elizabeth's expression was grim. "It's probably better she hears now instead of tomorrow when she has to leave."

Agnes was close to tears herself. "I think maybe the two of you had better leave so I can talk to Anya alone."

As they walked to the door, Mabel turned back to Agnes. "And to think he acted like there was nothing wrong. How he can get up there and preach on Sundays and pull a thing like this is beyond me."

With that, the two ladies nodded their heads in agreement and slipped out the door. Agnes closed it quietly behind them, then headed to find Anya. She had only taken a couple of steps when Anya came back into the room, still in her fishing clothes, tears streaming down her face.

Agnes looked at her. "Anya, aren't you going to change?"

Anya's spoke between breaths that came in quick burts. "I not change. I not go eat out. Anya prepare go home."

Agnes pleaded. "But Anya, you don't know for sure that is what he plans to do."

"You hear ladies. Men all same. Eli feel Anya not good enough, so send home."

Agnes could feel a tightening in her chest. "Maybe we could work it so you could stay here with us?"

Anya shook her head. "No. Anya not want be trouble for Eli. Eli say he have something important tell Anya. Anya tell Eli she go home so he not have to tell her."

Agnes felt her heart would break. She put her arm around Anya. "I'm sorry."

Anya was quiet for a moment. When she did finally speak, it was as if she was steeling her emotions against what lay ahead. She looked directly into Agnes's eyes. "Will do something for Anya, when Anya gone?"

Agnes nodded.

Anya quickly slipped off to her room. When she came back in, she was carrying the beautiful coat her mother had made. She held it out to Agnes. "Still want Eli have. Give him, after Anya gone."

Agnes felt her heart would explode inside her chest. "You really love him, don't you?"

Anya's voice quivered. "Anya not know. Anya never feel these feelings before."

Agnes put her arms around Anya and pulled her close. "I wish you would stay. I'm going to miss you."

Anya started crying softly. Her voice was soft and full of emotion. "And I miss you."

Chapter 24
The Storm

Eli stopped by city hall to get the book, *Pygmalion*. He thought they might like to finish reading it together after the big surprise. He patted his pocket. The money was there for dinner, as was the receipt from the captain for the gratitude dowry.

He couldn't wait to show the receipt to Anya and explain what it was. He could see it all now. They would be eating their dinner by candlelight. He would pull the receipt out and hand it to her. She would ask him what it was. When he told her what he had done, she'd throw her arms around him, and that's when he would ask her to marry him.

He locked the city building behind him and turned quickly toward Harris's home. That's when he saw them. Anya was walking straight toward him, with Agnes looming large beside her. Anya was still dressed in her fishing clothes, and he could sense something was wrong, but he didn't have the slightest idea what it could be.

As they approached each other, Agnes stopped and let Anya approach him alone. He smiled at her, but she did not return his smile. He put his arm around her, but instead of snuggling against him, he could feel her stiffen in his embrace. He held up *Pygmalion*. "I brought the book. I thought we might enjoy reading some more tonight."

Anya showed no emotion. Her voice was cold and monotonic. "Anya no want read book tonight."

Eli looked at her, but she turned her eyes away from him. He turned to look at Agnes, but her expression was rigid and unforgiving. "Why?" he asked.

Anya's face betrayed no emotion. "Anya no feel like read."

Eli looked desperately at Agnes, seeking help, but her expression remained cold and unchanged. He looked back at Anya, hoping for some explanation of what he was sensing, knowing things were spinning quickly out of control and he didn't know why. He tried to step where he could see her face, but she just turned farther away from him. He felt a desperation building in his heart, as he asked, "Are you just hungry? Do you just want to go eat?"

"Anya not hungry. "

Eli could feel the despair choking his voice, but could not control it. "Would you rather do something else? We can go for a walk, or anything you'd like."

Anya's voice was rigid. "Anya go home."

Eli stammered. "Oh, all right. I'll walk you home."

Anya turned and fixed her stare on him, looking right through him.

"No. Anya leave on ship tomorrow."

Eli looked away. "Oh." Then, suddenly, it dawned on him that she meant she was going on the ship and leaving for good. His head jerked up. "But I, um, thought you..."

Anya pulled away from him. "Anya go pack now."

Eli could hardly breathe. This had hit him so hard and unexpectedly. He took a deep breath, still hoping for some kind of explanation. "All right. I'll walk you home."

She turned back to him. "Anya fine alone."

And then she was gone. Agnes fixed one more glassy-eyed stare on him, spun on her heels, and fell into step beside Anya. Eli could feel his breath coming in short gasps and his heart pounding, as if it would tear from his chest. Before their conversation had ended, a few people had stopped to watch them. As he looked at them, he felt their look of condemnation, although he didn't know why. What had happened? When his eyes caught sight of Mabel and Elizabeth, he saw a strange smugness about them. There was a crack of thunder, and a heavy rain started to pour, sending everyone scurrying to their homes.

Eli felt very alone. He felt out-of-place, as if he had no home to go to. He didn't belong here. He felt he would suffocate as he gasped for breath from the pain in his chest.

He turned and ran. He ran blindly until his sides hurt; ran until his breath pulled hard from his lungs and would not return; and still he ran on. He ran until the pain screamed from his sides and legs, and the rain poured down his back and through his clothes. He stumbled and fell, and got up and ran some more. Finally, he could run no further, and he dropped to his knees and cried as his heart wrung with despair.

He didn't know how long he cried, but his whole body ached, and the cold shook him. He stood and found himself on the ridge where they had had their picnic earlier, and he fell to his knees and cried again. Eventually, he pulled himself under a little rock overhang, as the rain fell and the lightning flashed all around him. Its fury descended in full force. A wind started to howl and tear at everything around him. The whole force of nature hurled itself at the land and sea and everything on them.

By the time the rain abated, the sun was long down in the sky. Eli curled up and shivered. He knew if he didn't do something, he was going to freeze to death, but what? He didn't know how he would find his way off of the ridge without falling, nor did he have the energy to do so. He realized he didn't even care.

He watched the clouds continue to part until the north star shone bright and clear, directing sailors to their homes. But where was home? What was home? He sat alone, shivering. His thoughts were fleeting darts, dashing here and there. They darted to England and back. Then his mind just seemed to go blank.

Something seemed to call to him, and Eli struggled to pull his mind out of the abyss he was in. He started to ponder it all again. He thought to himself how much it had been just like with Molly. He hadn't seen it coming; he hadn't even guessed. Why was he so blind sided by this? What was it that he had missed? The harder he tried to understand, the more confused he became, so he sat there silently, in a quiet daze, letting time slowly slip away as his body stopped shaking.

He again felt his mind slipping away when he again thought he heard a voice calling him. He was freezing to death, and he was slipping in and out of a conscious state. He thought he must have imagined it, when he heard it once more, this time realizing it was Jim's voice. He looked and he saw a lamp bobbing along.

"Jim, I'm here!" he hoarsely called.

In no time at all Jim was beside him. He was concerned, but exasperated. "What in tarnation are you doing up here?"

Eli was so cold he could hardly answer. "Jim, I..."

Jim stopped him. "Don't talk now. Let's get you home first."

Jim put his own coat around Eli. He hefted Eli's arm over his old shoulders, helping him toward home. Eli found it hard to walk. His body didn't want to respond, and he wanted to just lie down. But Jim wouldn't let him, and as he forced him to walk, his body started to quiver and shake from the cold.

Jim knew the way home well, and moved them along the path easily. The walking made Eli's blood start to circulate, and the pain of cold became almost unbearable. It seemed to Eli like it took all night to get down to Jim's cabin, as the cold and pain wracked his body, yet as bad as that was, it paled in comparison to the pain in his heart.

Jim helped Eli get out of his wet clothes and wrapped him in a blanket. He fixed him a cup of warm tea. Once he knew Eli was going to be all right, he dropped into the chair across from him.

"Now you can tell me what made you go off and try to kill yourself in an icy rain storm like that."

Eli struggled to speak, as his voice didn't want to cooperate. "I just had to get away."

Jim sipped his own cup of tea, ready for a long story. "All right, what's the matter now?"

Eli looked away. "Anya decided she is going to leave."

Jim jumped to his feet with an uncharacteristic spryness. "You can't be serious!"

Eli threw up his hands. "I don't know what happened. We had such a beautiful day together, and then, when she went home to get ready to go to dinner, it's as if everything changed."

"Did you tell her about the money for the Gratitude Dowry?"

Eli shook his head. "I was going to at dinner, but I never got a chance. She said she didn't want to go to dinner, then she just left."

Jim's voice carried a tint of anger. "If it was me, I'd go get the money back from the captain."

Eli again shook his head. "I can't do that, Jim. The money is because I love her, not because I am accepting a gift. Besides, if it wasn't paid, she could never return home."

Jim dropped back into his chair. His spoke quietly. "I suppose you're right. What are you going to do for a ticket?"

Eli looked away. The thought of Anya leaving was hard, but he had said he would help her do what she wanted. "I'll talk to Whitman in the morning. I'll see if he'll loan me enough for her ticket and enough for me to go to Pennsylvania."

Jim choked slightly, but nodded. "I hate to see you go, but I realize you must."

They sat there silently, numbly. When Eli did speak, his voice sounded tired and discouraged. "Jim, how can a person grow to love someone so much in such a short time, and how could I be so wrong about thinking she could love me?"

Jim thought carefully before he answered. Eli could sense a far away longing in his voice. "I think we learn to love those we do things for. Your whole week has revolved around doing things for Anya. You couldn't help but grow to love her."

"But she has done nice things for me, too, and, apparently, she doesn't love me," Eli said.

Jim shook his head. "I can't answer that. Maybe the things she's been through have made it impossible for her to love you."

Eli breathed a heavy sigh. "I have thought and thought about everything I said all day, every action I've done, and I can't seem to find anything that would have caused her to want to leave."

In the lamplight, Eli thought he could almost see tears in Jim's eyes as he spoke. "I was that way when I lost Mary."

"What do you mean?"

Jim stepped over to look at Mary and Jimmy's picture. "I spent months trying to think what I had done that God would punish me by taking my sweet Mary and my little Jimmy. Although it was almost thirty years ago, I remember the night they died as if it were yesterday.

"I was sitting at Mary's bedside rocking little Jimmy. I would get up now and then and get her a new cool cloth to help her fever. I was sitting there real tired, fighting drifting off to sleep, when she reached out her hand and took mine. She told me she loved me and would be waiting for me when it was my time to leave this life. I grasped her hand tighter, trying to hold her to me, but she just smiled at me, closed her eyes, and was gone. Almost immediately, Jimmy went too. It's as if..." Jim paused, trying to get the words he had held in so long in his heart to come out. When he continued, his voice was choked with emotion. "It's as if she took Jimmy with her."

Eli looked at his old friend, shoulders hunched over, leaning heavily on the desk where the pictures were. It was almost as if, for a moment, his heart felt everything Jim had gone through those many years ago. He could feel the pain in his own heart burn even deeper, considering the loss that Jim had felt. "I'm sorry. You don't have to tell me if you don't want to."

Jim took a deep breath and continued. "No. No, it's good for me to talk about it. This is the first time I've been able to since then. Like I said, I spent many weeks trying to decide what I had done to offend God.

"Then, year by year, my sorrow turned to anger, then bitterness, then finally despair. I remember that night, Jimmy's birthday, I cried out that I could stand it no longer and I had decided to end it all. It was then that you stepped off the boat and needed a place to stay."

As Jim finished, his voice was quiet and gentle, and he turned to look at Eli. Eli looked up at Jim, and his own voice quivered with emotion. "You've been more than a friend to me. You've been like a father."

Jim hobbled over and plopped in his chair. "And you've been like a son. I hate to see you go, but I want you to do what you need to."

At that moment, Eli realized how much they both had changed. Jim had not been able to let go of Mary and Jimmy, and yet, now, he was willing to let go of Eli if it needed to be. He realized Jim's heart was full of hope of what the future could bring, and that hope helped Eli feel stronger, like he, too, could trust God in what lay ahead. Eli felt the tears slide down his face.

"Jim," Eli said, after they had sat quietly for a moment, "where are Mary and Jimmy buried?"

Jim was slow to answer. "I purchased a little piece of land up on Gray Rock Ridge. I put a little fence around it. I planted some trees and some lilacs. Oh, how Mary loved lilacs. They were her favorite flower. The little cemetery is totally enclosed; few people know it's there. It sits quietly, privately, alone in some big pines, but with a view across the whole ocean. It's the place where Mary and I used to go to watch the sunrise."

Suddenly, Eli realized where it was - the grove of trees on the edge of the cliff, that spot Jim had looked at so intently. It began to all fit together. The little path up from their cabin. The Sunday afternoon walks alone.

He had picked flowers for Anya there, and they had eaten lunch there while fishing. He had been so close and not even known.

That ridge was one of the most beautiful spots around. He looked over at Jim. "That's where you always walk on Sundays, isn't it?"

Jim nodded. Eli hardly dared ask, but he did anyway. "I'd like to go up with you tomorrow, if you don't mind."

Jim looked at Eli, his eyes searching him, looking right into his heart and soul, trying to understand Eli's feelings.

Eli spoke through his tears. "I feel like they're my family, too."

Jim nodded. They sat quietly for a moment. It was as if both knew the other's thoughts, and no words needed to be spoken. They were both thinking about Eli's departure the next day. Finally, Eli turned and put his hand on Jim's shoulder. "I'll write to you."

Jim smiled. "I'll do my best to write you too. I've learned a bit from your classes." Then Jim chuckled a little bit, like his old self. "In fact, I'd write you every week, if you promise not to marry the postlady."

Eli and Jim both laughed, and it seemed to revive their spirits.

Eli patted Jim's shoulder. "I'll come back and visit."

"I think you probably will." There was a pause, then Jim asked. "Are you planning to preach a sermon tomorrow?"

Eli stood as he answered. "Yes. It will likely be my last."

"What are you going to preach about?"

Eli thought a moment. He stepped to the window and looked out at the stars twinkling above. "I'm not sure yet, but I have some ideas. I've wondered why God allows us to go through these kinds of things. I thought of Abraham, being asked to sacrifice his son, whom he loved. Only when he showed his willingness, did God step in and stop him. Perhaps we must each be willing to give up those who are most important to us to show God we are worthy of them."

Eli continued to look at the stars. Jim joined him at the window and saw the north start twinkling brightly. They watched it together for some time as Eli remembered what Victor had said. "Well, we'd better get some sleep. We're going to have a long day tomorrow," Jim suggested.

"Thank you for being such a good friend, Jim."

"Thank you," the old man said, swallowing hard, "for being my son."

Then they slowly headed off to bed.

Chapter 25
The Cemetery

A cloudy Sunday dawned with a drizzling rain falling. The sky was gray and dreary, reflecting Eli's mood and feelings. With overcoats buttoned snugly under their chins, Eli and Jim headed to church early, as usual, to set things up.

As Eli sadly shook hands with those who entered for church, he knew this would be his last Sunday there, and he wondered if Anya would come. She did come, with Agnes, and she was dressed in her sky blue dress with the white sleeves. Eli thought she looked more beautiful than ever, in spite of her red rimmed eyes. Why was she suddenly so unhappy? Had she decided she couldn't live in this place, or was it just that she didn't want him? It appeared he would never know - Agnes kept herself between the two of them like some kind of buttress on a castle, and he was walled out.

When everyone had taken their seats, he could see that the crowd was as big as it had been the week before. The strange looks told him that he was in the dark about something, but he didn't have long to think about it, since everyone was waiting for his sermon. He gazed over the people he had grown to love during the last two years, and struggled to keep his emotions under control. Unsure of himself, he began.

"So many things have happened to me this week that I don't even know where to start. Last night, as I pondered some of the events, I decided that, sometimes, we are required to let someone we love go if we truly love them. It reminds me of a story my mother told me.

"Once there was a man who found two wild birds who had fallen from their nest in a mighty wind storm. The birds were badly injured. The man took the birds home and put them in a cage and carefully fed them each day. The birds grew healthy and strong. The man's small son watched as his father carefully tended the birds.

"Then, one day, the man took the cage outside and opened the door. The birds carefully stepped out and flew. 'But Father', said the boy, 'do you not love the birds?' 'Yes', replied the father. 'You cannot take care of something, day after day without growing to love it.' 'Then how could you just let them go?' asked the boy.

"The father did not answer immediately, but the two of them watched the birds circle in the sky. One bird circled wider and wider, and soon disappeared over the horizon, never to be seen again. The other bird enjoyed the sun for a while, but came back and landed on the man's shoulder and sang happily. 'You see', the father said, 'love is not love unless it is freely given. This bird is now mine and needs no cage to keep her with me. The other bird is not mine and never would be.' "

Eli moved over between Jim and Anya and looked back and forth from one to the other. "Whether in life or in death, sometimes we need to open the cage of whatever binds our heart and let go of those we love and trust God that, if they are ours, He will bring them back to us again some day."

He was sure it was the shortest sermon he had ever preached, but Eli felt he could say no more, or his heart would burst. He simply, sadly, bowed his head and said "Amen." There was a quiet amen from the congregation, as everyone seemed to sense there was more in his sermon than they were hearing. As was customary, Eli shook hands as everyone left the hall. Anya only glanced at him briefly as she passed, and then turned her eyes from him. She didn't even speak. Agnes only scowled at him.

When Whitman stopped to shake hands, Eli asked him to stay. Agnes and Anya went on without him. Whitman didn't seem to know anymore than Eli did, and was confused about it as well. He said Agnes and Anya wouldn't even speak to him. When Eli asked Whitman about borrowing the money for the tickets, Whitman pleasantly agreed. "I'd be glad to sign something, or whatever you want to assure payment," Eli offered.

Whitman shook his head. "If I can't trust you, Eli, I don't know who I can trust. I just wish you weren't going." Whitman gave him the money, and they visited briefly for a few minutes before Whitman hurried to catch up with Anya and Agnes.

Eli and Jim sadly put the chairs away, knowing it would likely be the last time they would have church there. They worked silently. They gathered Eli's remnant of books from off of the barren shelves and somberly headed home. The rain had stopped, but the clouds hung drearily in the sky. Eli stopped once to look back, and Jim paused with him. They never said a word. They didn't need to.

When Eli's books were packed, they started the hike up to Gray Rock Ridge. Jim led the way and knew every rock and tree. Eli now understood why the trail was there and why Jim knew it so well.

When they reached the top, Eli looked at the spot where he and Anya had eaten their picnic lunch. The storm had washed away any evidence of the wonderful time they had had only a day earlier.

They walked across a knoll and through a row of pines where Eli had seen lilac bushes - the little grove that Jim had gazed at so intently. There was a hidden path which ended in a small clearing. In the center, there was a white picket fence, surrounded by lilacs and well-trimmed aspen trees. The aspen leaves fluttered happily in the breeze. The cemetery was well kept, and it was obvious to Eli that Jim put a lot of love into this place.

The lilacs were blooming in purples, whites, and reds, and their scent drifted across the grounds and mixed with the fresh, salty breeze coming off of the bay. They walked through the small gate, and Eli could see the divided tombstone. On the left was engraved. "Mary (Madileeno) Solarno Smith. Beloved Wife and Mother. May You Sleep In Peace Until That Beautiful Dawn When Our Hearts Shall Be Reunited As One. Born April 12, 1864, Died February 27, 1902."

In the center, next to Mary's epitaph, Eli read, "Jimmy Braden Smith, Wonderful Son. Rest Well My Son Until That Day When I Will Again Hold You In My Arms. Born May 15, 1896, Died February 27, 1902." Then, Eli saw on the right side, "Jim Jamison Smith, Born July12, 1854." The death area was left blank, as was any description.

Jim saw Eli looking at it. "It's very sobering to know where I'm going to end up. Whether I live my life well or not, whether I'm a hero or a villain, whether I'm a great man or a scoundrel; when all is said and done, this will be all I will truly own in the end."

Eli's heart felt different than he could ever remember. In this quiet, sacred place, there was almost a transparent, yet still unseen, connection to the life beyond. He comforted Jim, "You will own this and the love of your friends."

Jim nodded. "Yeah. But there may not be a whole lot of them." They stood there quietly for a moment, then Jim spoke. "I've never brought anyone else here. I dug the graves myself, chiseling through the rock, and set the tombstone myself. I planted the trees and lilacs and built the little fence. You are the first one that has ever shared this with me. I know it sounds crazy, but I would often come up here to talk to Mary. That is partly why I always came alone."

Eli smiled at him. "That doesn't sound crazy at all. It feels kind of like they are here with us."

Jim agreed. "It does, doesn't it?"

The day was peaceful, and time seemed to stand still for a long time. Then Jim chuckled slightly. "I've often wondered what someone would write on my tombstone when I was gone. I thought I might just do it myself. Put something like, 'I told you I was sick.' I heard about someone who did that. Or, I thought I'd just put 'here lies the grouchiest old son-of-a-gun that ever lived.' Save someone else the trouble of having to do it."

Eli had such a soft spot in his heart for this old man that stood beside him, and he thought about how many the people of the town misunderstood him. Eli thought of a lot of things, but he just couldn't get what was in his heart to come out in words, so he patted Jim on the shoulder and said, "How about, 'A good man with a big heart. One of the best men who has ever lived.'"

Jim grunted. "I'm not sure anyone would believe that."

"But they don't know you like I do."

Jim stood there in silence. It was the first time that Eli had seen Jim without anything to say. An idea came to Eli. "I know where there are some beautiful wild flowers we can add to the lilacs. Let's get some and put them on the graves."

Jim nodded. Neither said anything as Eli led the way to the spot where he had often picked flowers for Anya. They each picked a beautiful bouquet. Jim added a few dandelions for Jimmy, saying that Jimmy would often bring them to him, calling them "Daddy Lions". Eli blinked back the tears as he envisioned Jim with Jimmy running by his side.

As they returned to the graves, Eli wondered how long Jim would be around. Would he get back to visit him from Pennsylvania, or would he be visiting Jim here in this cemetery? The thought made his heart ache.

They cut some lilacs to add to the bouquet, and then, with no word passing between them, they both set about trimming the grass around the graves. When they were done, they stuck the lilacs into the dirt next to them and gently laid the wild flowers in front of the stone.

Eli could see tears rolling down Jim's cheeks as he kneeled and laid the handful of dandelions at the center in front of Jimmy's grave. They sat there quietly after they arranged the flowers, until they heard the long, deep sound of a ship horn.

Since the cemetery sat right on the edge of the cliff, with trees on only 3 sides, the two friends had a clear view of the harbor and the ocean from within its silent borders. From there they could see forever. They stood and looked out over the cliff.

Jim's voice was quiet and somber. "That would be the cattle boat telling the crew and all others to prepare for departure."

No other word passed between them as they turned and headed on their way. As he stepped out of the cemetery, Eli softly shut the gate behind him and looked back one last time at the tombstones. He did feel like they were his family. He whispered, "Goodbye." Then he turned and was gone.

Chapter 26
Saying Goodbye

Fearing that Anya would get on the ship early, they made a quick stop at Jim's house for the gift Eli wanted to give her, then hurried down to the dock. Eli paid the captain for the ticket, then he and Jim sat on the crates, quietly waiting - no word passing between them.

Eli could hear the steady, yet consoling grind of the cattle boat against the dock. He looked up at the ship, the ship that would take Anya away. Somehow, it again seemed to be wanting to tell him something again - something he just couldn't seem to grasp.

The monotony was broken by Agnes's heavy footsteps, followed by the timid steps of Anya close behind. Anya was wearing the ugly dress she had come in and, apparently, they had fashioned her another veil, though it was not pulled over her face. Whitman was carrying her old bag, plus a new suitcase, presumably a gift from Agnes. Mabel and Elizabeth, throwing sideways scowls at Eli, quickly hurried over to Anya. Eli could see he was an outsider and would totally be ignored if he didn't push his way in.

When he approached Anya, all four women went silent. He felt awkward and unsure, but he had to say goodbye. He forced a smile. "Do you have everything you need?"

Anya did not return his smile. "Anya be fine."

"Is there anything I can do?"

Agnes stepped up, as if protecting Anya. "I think you've done quite enough."

Eli flinched, again getting the feeling that there was something he was missing. He steeled himself. He was going to do what he came for. "I have a present for you."

Anya finally looked at him. "Flowers?"

"No. Better than flowers." He held out the book, *Pygmalion*, to her. "We didn't get to finish it. I thought you might like to take it with you."

Anya nodded. "Thank you." They looked at each other for an instant, and then there were two loud blasts from the whistle of the ship. Anya backed a step away from him. "Anya must go now."

Eli stepped aside, and the women hustled Anya onto the ship, with Whitman close behind them carrying her bags. All of the women hugged Anya goodbye, and Whitman shook her hand. All too soon, the ship was untethered and heading out to sea. Everyone waved, although Eli couldn't see Anya anywhere on the ship. They waved until it had turned and headed south - until Eli knew she was gone for good.

Chapter 27
Learning The Truth

When the women and Whitman left, Anya fled to the other side of the ship. She felt like her heart would burst, and she could not bear to see Eli. She had been so sure he was different. Things had felt different when she was with him.

When he had put his arm around her she had felt feelings go through her that she couldn't describe. Yet, when it was all said and done, he had cast her away like an old rag because she wasn't good enough for him. He hadn't even thought she was worth any kind of gratitude dowry, and now, he was sending her home.

Home. What would happen when she got there? Would she be put to death? Would she disappear from the village like other women had? She suddenly felt very frightened, and she started to cry. She didn't even think she was afraid of death. She was more crushed by the feelings she had for Eli, only to be sent away. She would never see him again. She almost hoped in her heart that she would be put to death. She couldn't stand to be sold again. After the feelings she had for him, she would rather die than belong to someone else. She knew she could never feel about someone else like she had felt for Eli, nor could she ever forget him.

She sobbed until she didn't think she had any tears left in her. She didn't hear the footsteps until they were almost right beside her. She turned to see the captain standing there looking at her. She tried to compose herself and act like she was just looking out over the ocean, but she knew he could see how upset she was.

He leaned heavily on the railing by her. "I thought I might find you here. Why you not on other side of ship to wave to friends?"

"Anya sad. Anya not want wave."

The captain's voice was rough from years at sea and from the pipe smoke. "Me think you not want to leave."

Anya shook her head. "Anya no want leave."

"Then why you leave?"

"Anya no want be problem to Eli."

Victor looked puzzled. "What you mean? He say he love you."

Her eyes widened. "He say this? But Anya think Eli want Anya leave."

Victor's brow creased. "What make you think that?"

Anya turned sadly away again. "Eli send Anya home."

Victor's voice almost growled. "He no send you home. He buy ticket to United States for you to go to California."

Anya whispered, almost hoarsely, "To California? But I thought Eli send Anya home."

"He afraid to send you home. He said he wanted you to be happy, and you wanted to go to California."

Her mind raced. "But why Eli work so hard get money for Anya ticket? Sell many things. Ladies say Eli buy ticket yesterday because he want Anya leave."

Victor looked confused. "He no buy ticket yesterday. He bought ticket only this morning after you say you leave."

Anya gasped. "This morning? Then why Eli let Anya go?"

Victor let out a tired sigh. "Do you not remember the story of two birds? Man let go free. One fly away and not come back. It no love man. But other fly, then come back. It love man."

"What have do with Anya?"

"Anya is bird," the captain said. "Eli is man. Anya ask to go, so Eli get ticket to let Anya go free. He love you and hope you stay, but allow go free. Only you decide if you stay."

Anya began to grasp what Victor was saying, but she still couldn't believe it. "If Anya important to Eli, then why Eli not pay Gratitude Dowry?"

Victor stood up straight as he spoke. "What you mean?"

Anya's voice quivered with emotion. "If woman important to man, he pay Gratitude Dowry. Never have man no pay unless no want woman."

"But he did pay," Victor said sternly, looking her straight in the eye.

Anya looked at Victor, her mouth wide open. She breathed deeply a couple of times, then spoke quietly. "He did?"

Victor nodded. "Da. Yesterday he give me money for Anya's Father."

Anya choked slightly as the truth started to sink in. "Money for Gratitude Dowry? Yesterday?"

Victor reached in his pocket and pulled out a letter. "Da. He also give letter for your father."

Anya's voice trembled with emotion. "What letter say?"

Victor shook his head. "I no read. Letter's private."

"Please!" Anya begged. "Anya need to know."

Victor slammed his fist on the rail. "Not appropriate!" Then he looked down into Anya's face, her big brown eyes pleading with him. He let out a sigh and nodded. "Hokay, we read."

He slid his finger along the flap of the envelope, then pulled the letter out. He held it up, and with a quick glance at Anya, he started to read.

"Dear Anya's Family, I can not tell you how much I love Anya. She means more to me than any money can say. I am not a rich man, so I can send only a small amount of what I feel she is worth. Therefore, I give all I that have as that small token of how grateful I am to have her. Sincerely, Eli Whittier."

144

Tears were beginning to flow down Anya's cheeks as she remembered how she had treated Eli and what had happened over the last day. He had loved her and trusted her, and she had betrayed that trust by not returning it. Her heart tore at her and her breath started to come in gasps. "Anya not know."

Victor tried to comfort her. "Eli love you very much."

Anya, her heart wrenching within her, began to sob openly, the feelings of what had happened and her lack of trust in Eli breaking down the last of her internal strength. She forced herself to speak through her grief and shame for there was one more thing she had to know. "How much he send? He send dollar? Anya not worth more than dollar."

Her heart burned. Never had she felt as worthless as she felt at that moment.

Victor looked directly into Anya's face. "Anya worth more than dollar to Eli. That why Eli sell many things." He reached into his coat pocket and pulled out a small money bag and slapped it down on the rail. "Eli send fifty dollar."

Anya gasped and put her hand to her mouth, as the full realization of what had really happened yesterday hit her, and she understood the full truth of what Eli had done.

Chapter 28
Home

As the ship disappeared from view, disbelief and hopelessness filled Eli's heart. He had learned to love Anya more in that one short week than he thought he could ever love anyone. The ship turned heading south along the coast. Eli felt desperately like running after it. He would have gone to the ends of the earth to get her if he thought that she wanted him. But she didn't, and his heart filled with despair. Anya had made her decision, and it didn't include him.

As the ship faded from view, Whitman quit waving. "Well, there she goes."

Agnes dabbed her eyes. "I feel like I've lost a daughter."

The crowd that had gathered gradually started to fade away. Eli looked as if his world had been shattered. He turned to Jim. "Somehow I thought she might change her mind and stay. I thought she might ..."

He stopped, too overcome with emotion to speak. Eli blinked back his tears and swallowed hard to get his heart out of his throat, and tried again. "I just thought she might learn to love me and want to stay here."

Jim choked on his words. "I thought so, too."

Mabel stepped up behind Eli. "You mean you wanted her to stay?"

Eli couldn't speak, so it was Jim that answered in a strong, disgusted tone. "Of course he did!"

"Then why did you buy her a ticket?" Elizabeth asked. "Why did you let her go?"

Jim tapped his cane with impatience at her. "Don't you understand? It had to be her decision, not his."

Elizabeth and Mabel looked at each other, shock written on their faces. They looked over at Agnes who had an expression not only of shock, but also of anger, as she glared back at them.

Eli didn't notice. His heart was breaking as he spoke. "The passenger boat to the United States should be here this afternoon. I guess I should go and get my things packed."

Mabel stopped him. "You're not leaving?"

Again Jim spoke for Eli. "Eli needs to be where he can find a wife. All of the women here are too old or too young."

Eli turned and looked one last time out over the harbor, as if, somehow, it was all a bad dream. He shook his head. "It's strange. I thought today might be my wedding day, but instead, everything I wanted in life is gone. I guess I was wrong in thinking God had brought me here for some purpose, or..." he paused, looking at Jim, "perhaps if he did, it is time to move on."

Jim nodded, understanding what Eli was saying. Eli headed back to the cabin. Jim turned one last time to look out over the harbor. As he turned to follow Eli, Mabel reached up and grabbed his arm. "But why did he work so hard to get all that money if he wasn't planning to send her home?"

Jim angrily turned to face her, and she nervously stepped back a step as he spoke. "Eli never planned to send her home!"

"Oh, really?" Elizabeth said defiantly, stepping up beside Mabel. "Why did we see him buying a ticket from the captain yesterday?"

This time it was Whitman who answered in his characteristic drawl. "He couldn't have bought it yesterday. He borrowed the money from me this morning to pay for her ticket."

Agnes looked at the other two women, and then back at her husband. "He did?"

Mabel stammered. "But we saw him pay the captain yesterday, so..."

Jim's voice was angry and disgusted. He took a menacing step toward the meddlers, and they retreated a step or two. "Don't you women understand anything!? He wasn't buying a ticket. He was paying fifty dollars for the Gratitude Dowry to show how much he loved her!"

Agnes gasped. "Fifty dollars! But Anya said he only needed to pay a dollar."

Jim's voice trembled with emotion. "Eli wanted her to feel she was important and know he loved her. He didn't want to pay it as if he was accepting a purchase. He only paid it for Anya."

Whitman shook his head. "Well, it doesn't matter any more, because she's gone."

Jim's voice lowered and wavered as he turned to head home. "Yes, and soon Eli will be gone, too."

As Jim slowly, dejectedly, walked down the dock and turned out of sight at the end, the others watched him silently, dumbfounded.

Mabel wailed, putting her hand to her forehead, overcome with emotion. "I'm sorry. This is my fault."

Elizabeth's voice was heavy, as well. "Mine too."

Whitman turned and looked at them. "What do you mean?"

Mabel looked away, unable to face him. "Anya overheard us telling Agnes that Eli was raising the money to send her home."

Whitman shook his head, not comprehending what they were saying. "So?"

Agnes stepped up trying to explain. "It was before Anya had decided to leave."

Elizabeth joined her. "We didn't know he was raising money for the Gratitude Dowry. We thought it was for a ticket."

Mabel jumped in, speaking fast now. "When she felt Eli didn't want her, that was when she decided to go."

147

Agnes breathed heavy through tears of her own. "She really wanted to stay."

"If there was any way we could take it back..." Elizabeth started to say, but was interrupted by Whitman, who had finally grasped the situation.

"You mean she wanted to stay and marry Eli, but she thought he didn't want her?" The ladies could not look him directly in the face, but they all nodded. He looked back and forth from one lady to the next. He stopped at his wife. "What did I tell you about meddling in the affairs of others?" Whitman didn't say any more, seeing the tears already flowing down her face.

Whitman took a deep breath, and with an air completely unlike him, bellowed, "Ladies, we are going to stop that ship!"

Suddenly, the atmosphere on the dock turned from despair to excitement as he continued. "I don't have the rigging done on my boat yet, so we'll have to row for it. Mabel, grab some oars."

Mabel stepped forward and saluted excitedly. "Aye, aye, Captain." With that, she dashed off down the dock.

Whitman ordered resolutely. "Elizabeth, grab some rope."

Elizabeth saluted. "You've got it." And off she raced for some rope.

Whitman turned last to his wife, her tear-stained face looking lovingly at him. He was enjoying his authority. "With three women in a boat we'll need some life preservers. Agnes, grab some life jackets."

Agnes grinned and jumped to life. "I'm on my way."

Whitman started loosened the tethering on his small boat as the ladies came running back with the requested items. Whitman held up and oar as if giving a pep talk. "We will all need to row for all we're worth to catch them."

Agnes looked concerned. "What if they won't stop?"

Whitman frowned and spoke forcefully. "By George, they had better stop. I'm the port authority, and I'll have them arrested if..."

But his voice was drowned out by the long, shrill blast of a ship whistle. They all turned as a second whistle blew, and the cattle boat came into view around the bend.

"Wait a minute!" Elizabeth exclaimed. "Look! The ship, is coming back!"

They all started jumping and hugging each other in excitement, except for Whitman, who never got too stirred up about anything. Instead, he was annoyed at the others shouting around him. He was especially annoyed at Elizabeth, who had forgotten to drop both ends of the rope, and was dancing around him, tangling him up in her frenzy.

Mabel held her hand to her forehead so she could see better. "Do you think that maybe she..."

"Yes!" Elizabeth hollered. "Look! It's Anya. She's waving."

Elizabeth finally dropped the rope and started waving. "She must have decided to come back!

"Quick, go get Eli!" Agnes commanded.

Mabel and Elizabeth raced off, each trying to outpace the other in their flight to Jim's cabin. The ship was just moving into position by the time Eli came running breathlessly onto the dock hollering, "Hurry, Jim! Hurry!"

Jim came panting along behind him, moving spryly for an old man. "I'm a-comin'. I'm a-comin'. I'm not as young as I once was, you know."

Everyone chattered excitedly as the ship docked and the gangplank was lowered. Everyone went silent as Anya stepped onto the gangplank. She walked slowly, directly, deliberately down it and then toward Eli. She stopped a few feet from him, eyes lowered and ashamed. She looked as if she was going to cry as she spoke. "Eli pay fifty dollar Gratitude Dowry for Anya."

Eli nodded. "I wanted you to know that you are more important to me than anything. I wanted you to know that I love you very much."

Anya blinked back the tears and looked into his face. " Anya know. And Anya love..." She paused and smiled at him through her tears, and then very carefully and deliberately chose her words, "And *I* love *you*."

She ran into his open arms, clinging to him as he swept her off of her feet and swung her around. He kissed her, and her tears mingled with his own.

Finally, Jim tapped his cane impatiently on the dock, trying to break everyone from the trance they seemed to be in. "All right, already. Aren't we supposed to have a wedding or something? We can't just stand around here all day. Some of us got things to do."

Eli reached out and gave his old friend a kindly whack. "You old lumberjack, you. You don't have anything better to do."

"Nonetheless," Whitman said, "in order to come through customs, she must be married, and, since the preacher can't perform his own wedding, I suppose, as mayor, I will just have to do it."

By this time, word from Mabel and Elizabeth was spreading around the town, and a crowd was gathering fast. Whitman motioned to Eli. "Let's get the couple arranged up here." Once they were in position, Whitman began. "As mayor..."

Agnes raised her hand. "Hold on just a second."

Agnes trotted at a quick pace toward home. Whitman shook his head. "She's always interrupting me," he said, jokingly, to the laughter of the crowd.

After some time, Agnes returned, breathlessly, carrying the flowers Eli had given Anya the night before. Over her arm, she had the jacket that Anya's mother had made. "A girl needs flowers when she gets married, and Eli supplied them. And, I think, Anya would want this, too."

She held out the coat to Anya, who took it from her. Anya held the coat out to Eli. "This for you from my mother."

The crowd gasped at the magnificent colors of the coat. Eli took it from her. "It's beautiful. Thank you." He slipped his old coat off and put the

149

new one on as Anya beamed proudly at him.

Agnes also laid some books she had been carrying at Eli's feet. They were the books that Whitman had purchased from Eli. Agnes smiled at Eli and gave a strong look at Whitman. "I am also sure that Whitman wouldn't mind if I give these to you for a wedding present."

Whitman, not looking very enthusiastic, but catching the look from his wife, nodded. "Of course not." He turned back to the couple. "Shall we continue?" Agnes, Eli, and Anya nodded. Whitman cleared his throat and began again. "As mayor..."

This time he was interrupted by Elizabeth and Mabel, who had been whispering since they had seen the books Agnes had set down. Mabel held up her hand. "Hold on just a minute."

Whitman rolled his eyes as the two scurried off toward their respective homes. A few others caught the spirit and disappeared as well.

Whitman turned toward his wife. "I suppose next you will want to send out for punch and cookies?" and, winking knowingly at Jim and Eli, whispered, "I hope Anya doesn't make the cookies."

The crowd continued to grow, as did the stack of books at Eli's feet. Elizabeth and Mabel returned, and Elizabeth held the wedding dress up to Anya, and Mabel offered the ring to Eli. Eli protested. "But I can't..."

Mabel looked him in the eye. "They're yours now."

Eli shook his head. "But I sold..."

Elizabeth put her finger to his lips. "They are our wedding present to you."

"And," Mabel added, "our way of saying we're sorry."

Eli spoke quietly. "Thank you."

The ladies ushered Anya into a little fishing shack, and shortly they emerged with Anya wearing the wedding dress. They escorted her to Eli's side. As Anya smiled at him, Eli thought she had never looked so beautiful as she did at that moment.

Whitman cleared his throat. "Now are we ready?" The women nodded.

"As mayor and justice of the peace, and by the authority vested in me by the people of this town, these two are here with the desire to enter into the holy state of matrimony."

Anya turned to Eli, a look of confusion on her face. "Anya thought..." She paused a moment, then started over. "I thought we get married?"

Eli smiled at her. "Yes. That's what matrimony is."

She looked relieved. "Oh."

Jim scowled at Whitman. "Quit using high falutin' words, you old sea barnacle, and get on with it!"

Whitman grunted at Jim, then continued. "Do you, Anya..." He lowered his voice and spoke directly to Anya. "Anya, do you have a last

150

name?"

Anya looked puzzled. "I no understand."

Jim tapped his cane on the dock, quite annoyed. "She doesn't have one yet. That's what we're here for."

Chuckles were heard through the crowd. Whitman glared at Jim for stealing his moment, but he started again. "Do you, Anya, take Eli Whittier to be your lawfully wedded husband, for as long as you both shall live?"

Any nodded vigorously. "Yes! Yes!"

Whitman turned to Eli. "And do you, Eli Whittier, take Anya to be your lawfully wedded wife, for as long as you both shall live?"

Eli turned to Anya, smiled, and squeezed her hand. "I do."

Whitman motioned to Eli, "You may now put the ring on her finger."

Eli glanced at Mabel for permission, and, at her nod, put the ring on Anya's finger.

Whitman, enjoying his audience, spoke with a voice of authority. "By the power vested in me as the representative of the people, justice of the peace, mayor of..."

Jim tapped his cane loudly. "Quit braggin' and get on with it!"

Deflated, Whitman frowned at Jim again, but continued. "I now pronounce you man and wife."

Jim raised his cane in the air and shook it in triumph. "Take that, Molly!"

Victor stepped off of the ship and handed the money Eli had paid him for the ticket back to Whitman. He set down Anya's bags and set the book *Pygmalion* in the pile at Eli's feet. Satisfied, he returned to his ship. The gangplank was drawn in as Whitman finalized the ceremony. Speaking to Eli he said, "You may now kiss the bride."

Eli pulled her close and embraced her with a kiss, as two long, happy blasts on the ship's horn echoed the revelry of the crowd. The ship pulled away, heading out to sea, leaving Anya where she belonged.

The clouds slowly parted, and a single ray of sunshine shot through. The hole in the clouds kept growing wider and wider, as a rainbow arched across the sky, adorning the hillside and the town. It seemed as if all of nature was celebrating.

Eli held Anya close. He realized that home is ultimately found in a person's heart, and not merely in the place he lives. For in his heart he knew they were home. He and Anya truly were home.

If you liked this book, we'd love to have a review on Amazon if you have time.
http://amzn.com/1480200387

For copies of this book and other works
by Daris Howard go to:
http://www.darishoward.com

Other books
by
Daris Howard
Daris Howard Amazon page: http://amzn.com/e/B004H76UGK

Life's Outtakes books
(52 humorous and inspirational Stories in each book)

1. When The World Goes Crazy - Life's Outtakes Year 1
2. All's Well Here - Life's Outtakes Year 2
3. When Life Is More Than We Dreamed - Life's Outtakes Year 3
4. Nothing But A Miracle - Life's Outtakes Year 4
5. Singing To The End Of Life - Life's Outtakes Year 5
6. It's Ninety Percent Mental - Life's Outtakes Year 6

The Three Gifts
http://amzn.com/1449961436

Three young men are convicted of mugging little children for their Halloween candy. Instead of sentencing them to jail, as is expected, the judge sentences them to 100 hours of community service babysitting at the Women's Crisis Center.

They were prepared for jail, but they were not prepared for what was in store for them as the children opened their eyes and hearts and changed their lives.

Essence Of The Heart, The Royal Tutor -

http://amzn.com/1479392189

Mystery, Intrigue, And Clean Romance!

When he is called before the queen, Jacob, the handsome, young Captain of the Royal Guard, is sure it is to discuss the baffling increase in assassination attempts against the royal family. Instead, the queen assigns the shocked young captain to tutor her out-of-control, tomboy daughter, Marie.

He knows all of the other tutors have failed miserably, and he tries to beg out of it, but the queen will not relent. However, she does give him leave to use any teaching method he likes. Her ultimate command is that she be trained as a lady in preparation for her royal ball.

Angry and humiliated at what he feels is a degrading and impossible assignment, especially for a military captain, he determines to train the princess like he would one of his guardsmen. He will demand strong discipline, tough academics, and sword combat training. He is sure that his rigorous approach will push the princess to complain to her mother, who will then remove him from the assignment.

But to his surprise, Marie instead responds positively to the harsh discipline, and becomes a princess like no other.

And, when they come under attack, her training might be just enough to save both of their lives as they work to unravel who is behind the assassination attempts, and also try to solve the mystery of why the Lord High Chamberlain is such a great sword fighter.

About The Author

Daris Howard, an award winning author and playwright, grew up on an Idaho farm. He was a state champion athlete, competed in college athletics, and lived for a time in New York.

He has worked as a cowboy, a mechanic, in farming, and in the timber industry. He is now a college professor. He has also been a scoutmaster, having up to 18 boys in his scout troop at a time. In his wide range of experience, he has associated with many colorful characters who form a basis for his writing.

Daris has had plays translated into German and French, and his plays have been performed in many countries around the world.

For many years Daris has written a popular column called *Life's Outtakes* that consists of weekly short stories, and is published in various newspapers and magazines in the U.S. and Canada.

Made in the USA
Charleston, SC
01 April 2013